NOW

I leaned my head back. "Does Mom know?"

"I think she's sensed it. But we've never talked about it openly, if that's what you mean. Jean hates confrontation. Living by what other people think is much more important to her than it is to me."

I thought of the personals ad. Before this I'd been hoping it would work, but suddenly the thought of both Mom and Dad having partners seemed scary. I'd be all alone. No matter what Dad says, he loves someone else now. I'm not that important to him anymore. That hurts. He's just trying to soft-pedal everything, pretending everything will be the same. It won't be. It can't.

Other Bantam Starfire Books you will enjoy

THE SOLID GOLD KID by Norma Fox Mazer and
  Harry Mazer
TOO YOUNG TO DIE by Lurlene McDaniel
GOODBYE DOESN'T MEAN FOREVER by
  Lurlene McDaniel
WAITING FOR THE RAIN by Sheila Gordon
THE AMAZING AND DEATH-DEFYING DIARY
  OF EUGENE DINGMAN by Paul Zindel
US AGAINST THEM by Michael French
PEOPLE LIKE US by Barbara Cohen
MORNING IS A LONG TIME COMING by
  Bette Greene

Now That
I Know

Norma Klein

BANTAM BOOKS

NEW YORK · TORONTO · LONDON · SYDNEY · AUCKLAND

RL 5, IL age 12 and up

NOW THAT I KNOW
A Bantam Book

PRINTING HISTORY
Bantam hardcover edition / May 1988
Bantam paperback edition / September 1989

LIBRARY OF CONGRESS
Library of Congress Cataloging-in-Publication Data

Klein, Norma, 1938–
  Now that I know / Norma Klein
     p.   cm.
  Summary: Thirteen-year-old Nina has grown accustomed to
spending part of the week with each of her divorced parents until
she discovers the real reason for the breakup of their marriage.
  ISBN 0-553-28115-1
  [1. Divorce--Fiction.   2. Fathers and daughters—Fiction.
3. Homosexuality—Fiction.   4. Mothers and daughters—Fiction.
5. New York (N.Y.)—Fiction]   I. Title.
PZ7.K678345No   1988
[Fic]—dc19   87-32080
                                                            CIP
                                                            AC

Published simultaneously in the United States and Canada

PRINTED IN THE UNITED STATES OF AMERICA

O   0   9   8   7   6   5   4   3   2   1

To Mary Pope Osborne

Now That

I Know

1

"So, tell me," Dara said as we were walking home from school. "Do you want me to nominate you or not?"

I made a face. "We're only in ninth grade.... Do you really think I'd have a chance?"

The school Dara and I go to begins in kindergarten, but the high school is in a different part of the building. We've known a lot of the kids for years, but as high-school freshmen, we're suddenly the lowest of the low. School elections are in a few weeks, and the only job I've ever really wanted or cared about is becoming editor of the school newspaper, *Info*. Maybe I'm interested because of my dad. He's an editor of a medical newsletter. I've always liked the idea of thinking up articles, writing them, or helping others write them. Dad says that with a magazine or a newspaper everything matters: how it looks, the size of the type, whether or not you have illustrations. I've thought about it a lot since I was in younger grades. When they handed *Info* out to us I would examine every detail.

"Why not go for it?" Dara said. "You may not get it, but who knows, you might. Then you could get me to do the cartoons and illustrations. I think the ones they've been using are really dumb."

"Me, too." What I like about having Dara as a best friend is that her attitude toward *everything* is: go for it. At times her pushiness can be a pain with guys. Dara believes rejection is only scary when you think about it. I'm not sure. I think it could be bad both ways. I looked at her. "Tell me honestly, do you really think I'd be good? I mean, say you weren't my friend, would you want to nominate me?"

Dara is honest, too. I never ask her a question, unless I really want to know what she thinks. "No, I wouldn't be nominating you if you weren't my friend because I might not even know who you are! I mean, you *are* kind of quiet. I might know you if you were in my class, but not otherwise, is what I mean."

I felt discouraged. "So, maybe it's not worth it. If—"

"No, wait a sec. The point is, I do think you'd be good. You're great in English. Mr. Gainer adores you. He'd probably marry you if he wasn't married already! And you *can* be really organized if you want to."

It was nice of Dara to put it that way. I'm horribly disorganized about the subjects I hate, like math and chemistry (which I'm almost failing), but I think it's true: with things I care about, I'm different. Since my parents, especially Mom, are always going at me about my grades and how I'm not working up to my potential, this might make them both proud and also make them ease up on nagging me about college, which is almost four years away.

"Okay, Dara," I said finally. "Sure, do it."

"The whole point of high school," Dara said, "is that we *should* be doing new things. We're not babies anymore."

I knew she meant with boys, where I'm just about as inept as I am with chemistry. Dara's had boyfriends since she was in first grade. I'm not exaggerating. She was actually engaged to Wolf Rosen for a week when we were in first grade; he gave her a ring made out of a paper clip. Then she decided he was boring and broke it off.

We were at Ninety-eighth Street and Broadway, which is where Dara and I part every day after school. She lives at 104th and Riverside Drive with her mother, who's divorced like mine. I'm a J.C.K., a joint custody kid, which means I go back and forth, one week at Mom's, the next at Dad's. I felt weird about it at first, but now there are quite a few kids in our class who do the same thing. "See you," I called.

One major relief to me is that Dara didn't move to Vermont with her mom the way they were thinking of last year. Her mom, at that time, had a boyfriend who loved horses and had a farm, but when Dara and her mom got there, they felt this sudden yen for polluted air and muggers and excitement, and they decided to stay in the Big Apple. I know I should make more friends, but Dara and I know each other so well, it's really comfortable. Even when we get on each other's nerves, it's in a familiar way. Like she says, we know this is for life, so that makes any little fights we might have seem less of a big deal.

"Hi, Beautiful!"

Greg was in the kitchen, cooking as usual, when I came in. I threw my book bag on the floor. "Hi, Ugly," I said. That's our routine. He knows I don't think I'm beautiful and hate him to call me that and, actually, he's not ugly either. He's just kind of chubby for his age, which is the same as my dad's, thirty-four. He has frizzy brownish hair that stands up on end, and he wears these funny little granny glasses. I don't mind the style, but I consider them more for a kid my age than for an—you should pardon the expression—adult.

It's lucky my dad has a friend who not only likes to cook, but does it for a living. Greg runs this small gourmet health food store in our neighborhood, which is the Upper West Side of Manhattan. About five years ago our neighborhood really looked run-down, and now, all of a sudden, they're building all these high rises with health clubs in the basement. Dad says it's wrecking the neighborhood and taking away all the natural charm, but before, it was just big empty lots that looked like bombed-out shelters. Plus, as Greg said, now that more people with money live here, they'll be able to buy his health foods. That's what he's counting on.

I think it's good Greg can cook because both my parents, who've been divorced for about three years now (actually they told me on my tenth birthday, and

I've been thirteen for two months, so I remember it exactly), are lousy cooks. With my mom it's that she says she did cook when she was married and it was just drudgery, doing that on top of a nine-to-five job, so at her place we mostly just eat whatever we feel like, eggs or salads.

"You know, I was thinking," I said, sitting down at the kitchen table. I like watching Greg cook. Sometimes I help him with small tasks like chopping, if he doesn't want to use the food processor. "Maybe for Dad's birthday I'll surprise him and make him a whole dinner . . . if you can kind of help me."

Greg was tasting the stew. He goes by taste as well as by recipes. "Help, meaning I do the whole thing and you get the credit?" He grinned.

"No! Seriously, I'll do the whole thing, the chopping and everything. I just want you to be around so I can ask you questions if I need advice."

"What's the recipe?"

"I haven't picked it yet. But will you? If I do?"

"Sure. Your father will be amazed. He doesn't think you're the domestic type."

"I'm not." I glared at him. "Don't get the wrong idea. I'm not going to go around cooking from morning till night. I just thought I might learn a few basic things."

"Listen, Nina, I'm all for it. People who don't like food don't like life."

I snorted. I'm wiry for thirteen. I always had this horror of being a teenager, but now that it's upon me, as it were, it doesn't seem so bad. I'm the same person I ever was. It's dumb to think that because you reach a certain age you have to start acting like a different person—going boy crazy like Dara. She has a boyfriend a week. She's almost turned me off to the whole thing because I've noticed that practically as soon as she starts liking someone, she starts not liking him. Actually, I shouldn't criticize her because I'm the same way, only it's in my mind. Sometimes in the morning I'll think some guy in my homeroom is cute and by afternoon I've decided he's a complete jerk. I guess I'm either fickle or overly picky. Mom says it's better to be like that than do what she and Dad did, marry someone you meet in high school. This is hard to believe, but they actually met when they were fourteen and got married at eighteen. I can't possibly imagine falling in love with someone in my homeroom and actually wanting to marry him! I'd have to be desperate beyond belief to even contemplate something like that.

Mom says in her era if you weren't engaged by eighteen people thought you were a freak. Now it's the other way around.

"I thought I might look through Seventeen and pick something out," I said to Greg. "I have all these back issues at Mom's."

Greg put the stew in the oven. Then he started washing the pots and mopping up. "See what I'm doing now, Neens?"

"You mean cleaning up?"

"Right. . . . What I'm saying is, cooking isn't just cooking. It's the whole geschmear: buying the ingredients, checking to make sure you've gotten good values, making sure you have the right pans, cleaning up afterward. Follow-through. That's the key word. Like with your homework." He gave me a sideways glance.

That got me really irritated. I hate people lecturing me. Who is Greg anyway? Just Dad's friend. It's not like he's my father or my teacher or any person who's supposed to pester me about all that. I get enough of that from them. "Listen, I'm not a child," I snapped. "If you want to help me, okay. And if you don't, don't."

Greg used to be a teacher before he started this health food store. That may be why he has a tendency to lecture me. Plus he never had his own kids. It would be one thing if my own parents never did all that, but they do it from morning till night. Sometimes I feel it's *worse* if you're a kid from a divorced home. They're so afraid you won't get enough attention, especially about doing well at school, that you get *more* than you need. "I'm going to help, Neens," Greg said. "I told you. . . . How's the chemistry going? Need any explanations?"

I shrugged. Chemistry is a major sore point with me at this time mainly because I am, well, I hate to say this, but I might even *fail* it. And it's all my fault because chemistry isn't even a required course! I just took it because I had the completely erroneous assumption that it would be exciting. If you want to know where I got that idea, it was from Clark Ebberly, who was my best friend in third grade. He'd begged his mother to get him a chemistry set for Christmas and always used to be concocting things in his basement, weird magical-type things that smoked or turned beautiful colors. That's how I got the idea chemistry would be exciting and mysterious. It isn't. It's just memorizing formulas. The only halfway decent part is the lab and even that isn't that great. But the formulas are the pits.

"It's okay," I said. "I'll let you know if I need any help."

I hate asking Greg to help me. I'm afraid that I'll end up like Kelly Helms, who has a tutor for practically every subject in school. I don't consider myself dumb. I'd say I do have a tendency to put things off. There are just other things I enjoy doing besides studying. If Greg weren't around now, I'd turn on the TV and watch this soap that I always watch at Dara's house, *As The World Turns*. I know it's idiotic, but when you get home from a hard day at school, you want to unwind.

But since Greg was around, I flopped down on the couch and started leafing through some of the medical magazines Dad gets. I don't read the whole magazine usually, but now that Dara's going to nominate me for editor, I decided to go through to examine which ones seemed well laid out or eye-catching, and what kind of headlines might make readers curious to stop for the articles. The subject matter can be pretty dull or gruesome, with photos of people in various stages of getting horrible diseases, but the writing can still be surprisingly involving, almost against your will. Sometimes at night I remember some of those photos and wish I hadn't ever seen them. "What are you getting him?" I asked.

Greg was sitting in a chair reading, his apron still on. "It's a surprise."

"I won't tell him. I promise."

"I'd rather not. . . . You'll both be surprised."

That made me wonder if it was something for the apartment. Dad lives on the bottom floor of a brownstone on West Ninety-ninth Street, with a little garden out back where he plants stuff. He has a room for me that is also kind of his study. I'm at Dad's from Thursday evening till Sunday evening, and then I'm at my mom's from Sunday to Thursday. Supposedly if Mom had a real exciting social life, she could get all that out of her system while I was over here, but I know for a fact she mostly sits home and knits or goes to old movies by herself. She's worse about guys than I am! If some man has one tiny fault she says, "Why should I bother?" or, "Who needs that after a long day at work?" Her best friend, Sheila, says with that kind of attitude Mom's chances of remarriage are really small. Mom says, "So what?"

I would like to think my parents aren't bitter about splitting, but the fact is, they are. They think they wrecked each other's lives, Mom more than Dad. It's not one of my favorite topics. They got me out of it and, the way I look at it, they ought to make the best of it and look to the future.

That's what I tell them, but they don't always listen.

2

Dara thinks Greg is cute. When I asked Dad if she could sleep over Saturday night after going to the movies with him and Greg, she got manically excited. "Listen, he's thirty-four," I said, "and you're thirteen."

"So? There's this guy I met when we were in Vermont who's twenty-two and he said he thought I was fantastic. Seriously. He wanted to take me out, but Mom said no. I'm extremely mature for my age."

By that she probably means having big tits. How is that mature? Mature is in your head. "Look, if you're going to act like a jerk, don't come, okay? Because he's my father's friend and I don't want him thinking I have rotten taste in whom I hang out with."

"Thanks a lot." Dara sounded furious. "I know how to handle myself. Does he like women?"

"Yeah, he likes women. What a stupid question. Just not teenage kids. You want him to end up in jail?"

"Was he ever married?"

"No, but he used to live with someone, Myra someone. They're still friends." I wish Mom and Dad could be like Greg and Myra. I've heard Greg talk about things they still do together. Maybe that's because they weren't actually married. It's a lot better attitude than Mom's.

"So, do you think they might, like, get back together?"

"Myra and Greg? No! It's totally over."

"Meaning he's free?"

"Dara, you're really turning into some kind of sex maniac, you know that? Just because he's not married doesn't mean he's free or interested in a thirteen-year-old."

"Okay, just tell me one thing: Does he have a girlfriend?"

"Not that I know of."

There was a pause.

"So, do you promise to act regular and not like a fool?"

"Sure. . . . Can I wear my green wig?"

"Wow! Did it come? You didn't tell me." Dara ordered a bright green wig from a catalog her mother got. She's been waiting for it for ages. The reasons she did it are one, her hair is pretty short, and two, she wanted to stand out in some unusual way.

"It's just fantastic," she said, excited. "I look like a totally different person."

"Are you going to wear it to school?"

"Maybe, if I get the courage. But I thought I'd try it out on you first."

I was sure I'd think it was terrific, but I wasn't so sure about my dad's reaction. I guess if I had to describe my dad, I'd call him preppy, except that's kind of an insult, implying he's conformist and rigid. He isn't, really. Or rather he is in some ways, but I think it's because he grew up in a small town in Iowa. The kinds of clothes he feels most comfortable in are jeans or chinos, and checked shirts. I used to get him these wild-looking clothes for his birthday to jazz him up a little—polka-dot ties or straw hats—and he'd say politely, "That's really imaginative, Neens," and then put them in the back of his closet.

Then I figured, just like I have a right to my taste, which may not be his, he has a right to his, which may not be mine. Live and let live.

Greg is a little looser. Not what I'd call a great dresser, but still he does have a few fabulous items I'd love to borrow, like this cowboy belt and a neat sweater with all kinds of zigzag stripes. I wasn't sure if I should prepare them for Dara and her wig or not. Sometimes if you make too big a deal about something, it backfires. I decided not to.

Dara lives only two blocks from Dad's. When she rang the bell, I was in the bathroom so Dad opened the door. Greg must have been right behind him. "Hey, fantastic!" I heard Greg say.

Dara blushed. I could tell all her fantasies of an "older man" were starting up again. "Do you like it? I just got it from this catalog. I've never worn it before."

"It's super," Greg said. "It looks like Ethel's, doesn't it?" he asked Dad.

"Sort of," Dad said stiffly. It's hard to imagine one of Dad's friends knowing anyone who would be caught in a green wig.

"Nina was afraid you'd mind," Dara said, sort of playfully, to Greg. "You know, think it was too far out."

"Not at all. Why not let it all hang out occasionally?"

"That's what I think," Dara said, pleased.

I guess I'm more like my dad. Not preppy, definitely, but I don't especially like standing out, although I admire those who do. I don't like vivid colors like Dara wears, bright red or purple. I prefer subdued shades like gray or black.

In the movie, Dara maneuvered it so she sat next to Greg. Dad was next to Greg on his other side, and I was on the end next to Dad. When Dara got up to get popcorn, I whispered to him, "Do you mind?"

"About what?"

"The way Dara looks."

"No, it's fine. Not my taste, exactly, but you aren't about to do anything like that, are you?"

"Uh-uh!"

The movie was one of these old forties musicals that Dad and Greg like. It was in black and white. I never used to get the point of black and white. It seemed so drab after color, but Dad has made me see how it's beautiful in a different way. I also used to think the kind of tap dancing they did in those movies was dumb, and I hated the way all the women were always wearing huge hats and swishing their hair around. But maybe once you get used to something it doesn't seem as weird. Now I like it. We stayed for both movies. I glanced over at Dara to make sure she wasn't doing something awful like putting her head on Greg's shoulder, but she was okay. Sometimes she'd whisper to him, but that was all.

There's one really sad thing in Dara's life. It's not just that her parents are divorced, but her father, who now lives in Nebraska, has a new family. He told Dara on the phone when she called him last Christmas that he never wanted to see her again. Her parents got married real young, like mine. But imagine a person's own father saying something that awful? It would be the most horrible thing I can imagine. He must be a terrible person. Luckily, Dara's mother is really nice and they get along, but still, to me that doesn't make up for it.

When we got out of the movie we ran into Greg's former girlfriend, Myra. She was with a guy and she waved, and they chatted a little bit. Afterward, as we were getting into the car, Dara said, "Was she your girlfriend?"

"Yeah," Greg said.

"That's good that you're still friends," Dara said. "My mom and dad hate each other's guts now that they're not together."

Then Dara told them about how her father said he never wanted to see her again. "He sounds sick," my dad said.

I half minded Dara's telling them the story because I knew she just wanted to get attention, but still, maybe if something like that happened to me I'd want to tell people too. Or maybe the opposite. I might want to tell no one. "He *is* sick," Dara said vehemently. "If I could press a button and kill him without anyone knowing, I would. And I'd kill his wife and his kids, too, because they're all just as mean as he is."

"That seems a little extreme," Greg said, frowning.

"It's not," Dara sputtered. "They'd do the same to me. You don't know them. If you haven't met people like that, you can't imagine they exist."

Greg looked thoughtful. "No, I can. I've had plenty of major battles with my parents. I know what it's like. But I still think in the end it's best if you really try—"

Dara turned away, looking like she was going to cry. "I do! I *have* tried."

Greg reached over and put his arm around her. "Well, just keep trying, then."

She looked up at him and smiled through her tears.

When we got home, Dara and I got some ice cream from the freezer and took it into the garden. It was cool, since it was March, but not too cold to eat outside. "He is *really* nice," she said dreamily. I didn't have to ask if she meant Greg. "Some things are so unfair! Here it's like you have two fathers, Greg plus your regular father."

"I don't think of him as my father," I said.

"Yeah, but he's here. You can ask him about stuff. Mom has lots of boyfriends, but they're never . . . I guess it's that they usually have their own kids, so basically they tolerate me because I come with the package, so to speak."

If you put Dara's mom and mine in a bag, you'd end up with two normal divorced mothers. Dara's mom, Madge, is extremely attractive. She has one semi-permanent boyfriend she bought a house with on Fire Island, and even though they see other people, she still uses the house. Then she's got Harry, the guy in Vermont, which is where Dara met that twenty-two-year-old guy she thinks has a crush on her, although that's not much of a thing anymore. Plus she has just regular dates whenever she's in the mood. "It kind of evens out," I said, "because your mother at least has her own life. She's out there doing things. I feel like Mom just has me and most of the time, when I'm not around, she's just moping around the house, cursing her fate. I worry about what will happen when I go off to college."

"Yeah, I know what you mean," Dara said. She still had her green wig on, but now she yanked it off and placed it beside her. "My mom says no one is going to create a social life for you. You have to go out and do it for yourself. Although these days you have to be careful."

"Right." I picked up the green wig and began stroking it like it was a stuffed animal.

"Your mom's pretty," Dara said. "I think she is. Don't you?"

"Yeah." I didn't add another thing: I've seen Mom in the bath and she has a truly excellent figure, not just for someone her age, but for anyone, period. "Only, one, she's shy, and two, she's sort of bitter about men, because of being divorced."

"Boy, she should have been married to my dad!"

Dara said. "Your dad is nice, at least. Anyhow, like Mom says: Sure, a lot of guys are shits, but there are some nice ones, too, sprinkled here and there. You just have to look hard to find them."

I sometimes wonder about that in relation to myself, too. Where are all the good guys? I'm certainly not desperate about it, and I think lots of guys at my school are cute from a purely physical point of view. But when you think of wanting someone to talk to, forget it. They're just fools, most of them. I don't think it's that Mom's bitterness has worn off on me. I really don't. Dad says it's that boys my age are just less mature than girls my age, in every way. I think that's true.

After we finished the ice cream, Dara and I crept into my bedroom. Dad and Greg were sitting in the living room, talking. "Sleep well," Dara called out, waving her wig at them.

3

In school Monday Dara nominated me for editor. Martina Weiss seconded the nomination. I like Martina, but I don't know her too well since she just entered our class this year. Her parents are divorced too, but she told me that she gets along really well with each of them. She used to live with her mom, but this year she decided she wanted to go live with her dad. They said fine. Her parents are totally relaxed about all that.

Martina's pretty, but in a different way than Dara. Dara is more dramatic, both in the way she dresses and acts. It's obvious Dara wants to get people's attention and she usually does. Martina is small and blond, with a quiet voice. She makes her own ceramic jewelry, which she sells at a small store in Greenwich Village near where she lives.

After Martina seconded Dara's nomination I realized there was no turning back. Actually, it's not being editor that scares me, even though it does mean I'll be in a position of authority over older kids and boys. What scares me most is that every person who runs for anything, from school president to editor, has to get up at an assembly and give a speech telling why they'd be good for the job. I figure that the younger you are, the more the speech counts, since not as many people know you. I have a quiet voice. One reason I think I've never been cast in plays is no one can hear me. I'm really going to have to work on my speech.

At lunch time I thanked Martina for seconding the nomination.

"I just think you'd be great," she said.

"I'm nervous about making a speech," I said, biting my lip, a nervous habit I have.

"We'll help you with it. Won't we, Dara?" Martina always acts nice to Dara, but not so much the other way around. Dara is really jealous when I act friendly to other people. I think that's stupid and I've told her so. She'll always be my best friend, no matter what.

There are two other kids running against me, including one eleventh grader. I'm scared one of them will win.

Mom's birthday is two weeks after Dad's. I'd thought of getting her a piece of Martina's ceramic jewelry. Martina brought some pins into school, because Mom doesn't wear bracelets or necklaces. She makes humorous pieces of jewelry: three alligators hanging upside down on a branch or laughing hippos in various psychedelic colors. During lunch period Dara came over to look at them with me. "I have a better idea," she said.

"What is it?" I asked. I knew Dara just wanted to horn in and make me get Mom something she had suggested rather than something Martina made.

"You remember the other night how you were saying your mom never goes out, never has dates or anything, and you were worried about her?"

"I didn't say I was worried so much, but go on."

Dara looked excited. "Well, here's something my mom did once and it worked really well. She placed an ad in this personals column in the paper and she got responses. Lots of them! The best part is you don't have to answer any you don't like."

I crumpled the paper from my egg salad sandwich into a ball. "Mom would never do that in a million *trillion* years."

"That's where the present part comes in. You do it *for* her! You put an ad in the *Voice* saying, 'My mom is really terrific, extremely pretty, a good figure, smart,' all that, and then you pick out the best guys who answer and give her those letters as a present!"

Martina and I sat thinking about it. "I don't know," I said.

"It might be a good idea," Martina said thoughtfully. "Just to get her going."

"I don't know if she *wants* to get going," I said glumly.

Dara was eating only an apple. She's always on a diet. "But what if you get someone fantastic, like Greg? She could just marry one of them and it wouldn't be any trouble at all. Plus, you'd have the satisfaction of knowing you'd helped her out."

"She says she doesn't want to remarry, ever," I said. I wish Dara didn't have so many clever ideas. Mom feels men have let her down. I'm not sure she wants to meet a new one.

"But that's just because—like you said—she's feeling hopeless. She thinks there's no one out there. She thinks all guys are jerks."

At that remark two boys in our class, Todd and Matt, passed by and said, "Let her meet one of us."

Dara gave a loud derisive snort. "Drop dead," she yelled cheerfully. With Dara you never know if she's flirting. Even when she's saying awful, insulting things to boys, she kind of grins like she doesn't mean it.

"I'll think about it," I said. I looked down at Martina's pin with the alligators. "How much is that one?"

"Usually I charge ten, but you could have it for five," Martina said.

"Okay, well, maybe I'll get her that and I could still have money left over for the ad, if I decide to do it."

I wish Dara didn't regard it as a betrayal for me to like Martina, even a little. It would make my life easier. That's one reason I don't want to marry for a long time. I want to make sure I can really settle on one person. That's not the reason my parents broke up, though. Neither of them met anyone else. In some ways I'm glad that's true, but in other ways it makes it harder to explain their breaking up. They say their characters didn't mesh or something.

I kept thinking about Dara's plan. My mom is touchy on the subject of men and we have our ins and outs anyway. I didn't want to do anything that would make her mad. On the other hand, I could see Dara's point. Mom is shy, and this way if I could find someone perfect, it would save her all the trouble of going out and making small talk. In a way it would be like finding a job for someone who was unemployed without their having to go for job interviews.

I walked home after school. Mom's apartment is on 112th and Broadway, closer to our school. I still had time to watch TV, set the dinner table, and start my homework before Mom walked in. I know her schedule. I'd say her average time of arrival at our apartment is anywhere between 5:17 and 5:27. "Hi," I said. I hadn't seen her since Thursday morning. "How was work?"

"Rotten," she said cheerfully. "Did you put the potatoes in?"

"Oh, no, I'm sorry." At Mom's I'm supposed to check the refrigerator for a note that says turn on the oven, or whatever.

"We'll just have a veg, then," she said. Mom is erratic. She can hit the ceiling about some things and other times not care at all. The trouble is, I never know which mood she'll be in.

She went in to watch the evening news. Mom would like me to watch the evening news with her. She feels I don't know much about the world, especially facts about events outside the United States. This is partly true, but the times I've watched the news with her, it's so depressing I don't know how people can stand it. It's only at the very end that they have some human interest story about a whale that had twins that doesn't leave you feeling totally suicidal.

I don't think it's such a great idea for Mom to watch the news either, to tell the truth. She often comes in to dinner all upset about some horror story about kids on drugs and she'll start cross-examining me. Any story about teenagers gets to her in a hurry. She's sure whatever they're talking about is happening right at my school. Usually I have to spend half of dinner calming her down about it.

This time, as I was slathering catsup all over my hamburger, she said, "Those poor parents!"

"Which ones?" I tried to swallow what I'd bitten off so I could talk properly. I take too big bites if I'm hungry or we're having something I like.

"There's this little boy who has AIDS in some school in the Midwest, and one group of parents don't want him to go to school with their kids. So they've actually taken their kids out and put them in a separate school. Can you imagine how that kid must feel? It's not even his fault."

"Yeah, that sounds dumb," I agreed. Parents always seem semihysterical to me about a lot of needless things.

Mom was sipping her ginger ale. She never has wine or beer, as Dad does. "On the other hand, I can sympathize with the parents. It's their child, and who knows, there could be a danger. No one really knows."

Because I'd forgotten to turn on the oven, instead of potatoes we were having peas. I'm not crazy about vegetables in general, but I speared a few on my fork.

"One thing I'm not going to be when I'm a parent is hysterical," I said.

"Oh, you're not, huh?" Mom said. "You're going to be calm, cool, and collected every inch of the way? You're not going to care if your child dies or fails out of school or does idiot, destructive things to wreck his or her life? Well, let me tell you, you *are*! And if you're not, you'll be a lousy parent!"

Whew! "Mom, I didn't say I wouldn't be *concerned*. I said I wouldn't be *hysterical*."

"Look, who is hysterical around here?" Mom yelled. Obviously I had gotten her going. "I know you're failing chemistry. I got that letter from the school. So do you see me screaming or yelling? No! It's your life. You can fail any subject you want and get into a rotten college and have no job opportunities!"

"I got an 80 on my chemistry quiz," I screamed back. "I got it back today. Besides which, you say *you* went to a good college and you hate your job, so what does that prove?"

"It proves I have a rotten job," Mom said. "Do you want to find me a better one?"

Mom is an administrative assistant at a company that makes plastic beach toys. I know jobs are hard to get, but it seems to me if I had a job I hated, I'd at least look. At that point the phone rang. Mom got up to answer it. She said, "No, Mrs. Holley, Dara isn't here. I don't know *where* she is." She cupped her hand over the phone. "Do you know where Dara is, Nina? It's her mother."

"I think she went to the movies," I said.

"Nina thinks she's at the movies." Mom cupped

her hand over the phone again. "Do you know which one?"

"Something with James Dean, down in the Village, I think."

Mom repeated this message. When she hung up, she said, "Don't those two ever communicate? She calls here every other day."

"It's not Dara's fault," I said. "It's just her mother's out a lot so she doesn't have a chance to see her and tell her her plans."

"Out doing what?" Mom asked with a snort.

"With guys, going on dates. You know."

Mom laughed grimly. "No, I don't. What's a date?"

I started thinking of Dara's plan. "Dara's mother admits lots of guys are jerks, but she says there are some really terrific ones out there if you look hard enough."

"Spare me," Mom said. "That part of my life is over, thank heaven."

"Why?" I asked. "It's like with your job. You don't even try."

Mom turned red. "Look, you. You're—what? You're thirteen years old. You've had zero experience of the world, and you're giving me advice on jobs, men . . . Go out there and live and come back and tell me about it!" She flounced out of the room.

I felt rotten. I know my mom has a hard life. Even her best friend moved to California, so she doesn't have someone to talk to or hang out with the way Dad does. I can understand the mood she's in because I get in that same mood myself. Like, one thing goes wrong so you start thinking everything in the world is going to go wrong. Maybe I don't help. Sometimes I wonder if Mom would be better off on her own without the extra burden of a kid like me to worry about. On the other hand, maybe having me around is a kind of distraction.

By the time I finished with my homework, Mom emerged from her bedroom in her nightgown. "We never had dessert," she said.

"Is there any?" I said hopefully.

"I got some eclairs," she said with a smile. Those are my favorites, the mocha kind. At first we sat in the kitchen eating quietly, then she said, "Hon, it's just that I don't want you to repeat my life, marry the first guy who looks at you cross-eyed, settle for the first job. I want you to question things, be critical."

"Mom, I am. If I have any problem, it's that I'm too critical."

"You can't be too critical. Hone your critical judgment. Look at things as they really are, not as you want them to be. That's the key."

"One thing I forgot to mention," I said. "Today Dara nominated me for editor of *Info*, you know, the school paper. I don't know if I really have a chance, but—"

"Sure you do," Mom said. "It's all a matter of attitude. If you think you'll win, you'll win. Look at all those articles and essays you did for Mr. Gainer. He told me he thought you were one of his best students, ever."

I felt embarrassed. "Yeah, well—"

"Nina, that's why I don't get it when you just goof

off, like with chemistry. When you want to, you can do things so well."

"Mom, I'm just not good at everything, that's all. No one is."

"Just try!"

"I do. . . . Aren't you pleased, though, about the editor thing?"

Suddenly Mom leaned over and hugged me. "Of course I am. That was really nice of Dara to nominate you."

I hate to think of how much I want to win this thing. That's the trouble with running. When Dara first mentioned it, I thought: Why not? Now it means a lot to me, too much maybe.

4

I worked out my speech. Since I contributed articles to the paper last year I feel I know some things that could be done better. Everyone's always handing articles in at the last minute and then the editor doesn't have time to select the best. He or she has to just publish whatever they can lay their hands on. Also, visually the paper has been not that great. There's one girl, Beverly Jackson, who does all these cartoony little drawings and, to me, that makes the paper look babyish, not like a high-school paper. I think the guy who ran *Info* last year liked Beverly so he never even would consider anyone else doing the drawings. I know this because Dara asked him if she could try, and he said no. He didn't even give her a chance.

Maybe this is how politicians feel. What I mean is, I was glad Dara nominated me just because it was an honor, even if she is my friend. But now that I've started thinking about it, I really think I might be able to do a good job. I'm not sure I'd necessarily be better than the other people who are running, but I can see how I will give it my all. I also think I would like to prove to Mom that I can handle something that takes responsibility and organization without goofing off.

Plus, if I do fail chemistry, it'll seem to college admissions people that I was at least involved in extracurricular activities.

When I came over to Dad's on Thursday, it was after six. He was sitting alone in the living room. There weren't any delicious smells coming from the kitchen the way there usually are. "Where's Greg?" I asked.

"Oh, he's out seeing some friends from high school," Dad said. "Why don't we just order a pizza? What do you say?"

My dad is in good shape. He's neither too fat nor too thin, but he really is indifferent to nutritional values. Sometimes I nag him about it. We had a course last year and we studied how important it is to get certain vitamins. Dad never bothers with all that. Of course, when Greg is here to cook, he does get the right foods. Dad is fully grown, so I don't worry about him that much. I just think he should be more aware.

While we were having our pizza, I asked if I could practice my speech. "Time me, Dad. It's not supposed to run over ten minutes," I explained.

We went into the living room and I stood in front of the fireplace while Dad sat on the couch about eight feet away. "I realize I'm only a ninth grader," I started, "but I still think I can do a good job as editor of *Info*. These are some of the reasons why."

"Neens, why start off with an apology?" Dad said. "They know you're in ninth grade. That doesn't really matter."

That rattled me. "Well, it may not to you, but most people think the job should automatically go to a tenth or eleventh grader. Anyway, Dad, could you not interrupt me until I'm done? Just write down on a piece of paper what you think I should change."

"Okay." He got a sheet of paper and a pencil.

I decided not to write my speech out word for word, but to use a bunch of index cards that list my main points. Otherwise I might totally blank out in the middle. While I was talking, I sometimes looked at Dad and sometimes didn't. Of course I'd be more nervous talking in front of the whole assembly, but the way Dad stares at me very intently is also unnerving in its own way.

When I was done, he said, checking his watch, "Twelve minutes. Pretty good. I like it. It's convincing. I wouldn't talk quite so fast, especially at the beginning. I could understand you because I'm so close, but you swallowed some words in a way that could make some listeners tune out."

"I'm nervous!" I said, laughing.

"I know. But everyone is. The art of speaking is to make it appear that you're not nervous."

I sat down next to him. "Did you ever run for anything in high school?"

Dad looked off into space. He half smiled. "I almost did. . . . I almost ran for president of my class in tenth grade."

"How come you didn't?"

"Well, my best friend, Joey, was nominated and I wanted him to win, so I dropped out."

I was surprised. "You wanted him to win more than you wanted to win yourself?"

"In a way. I thought it meant more to him."

"Was it that you thought he'd be mad if you ran against him?"

"Not exactly. Maybe I really didn't want the job all that much. I didn't see myself as a leader, somehow. I still don't."

"So, did he get the job?"

Dad smiled. "Yeah . . . and he was good at it."

"Are you still friends with him, the way Mom is with Sheila?" That's Mom's friend in California, the one she's known since she was ten.

"No, we somehow . . . no." Dad trailed off, looking pensive.

I looked at him intently. Dad and I don't have a chance to talk alone that much because Greg is almost always here. I realized that I liked just the two of us alone for a change. Dad and I don't get into the kind of bristly fights over little things that I do with Mom lately. "Is Greg your best friend now?"

Dad nodded.

I lay down on the couch and put my feet in Dad's lap. "In a way I like it with Greg not here," I admitted. "I like it being just the two of us."

"Really?" Dad looked concerned. "Don't you like Greg?"

"I like him," I said. "Only when he's here I have to share you with him. We can't have talks like this."

"That's true," Dad said. He looked worried. "I hadn't thought of that."

"Maybe this is just a kid's point of view," I went on, "but if there are two grownups, they tend to talk to each other. It's not that they want to be mean. Maybe two kids do that also. But I don't always have a friend over so—"

"You're right," Dad said. "I didn't think of that. I'm glad you brought it up."

I was really glad we were having this personal conversation. It made me feel grown up. "This might sound contradictory," I said, "but I sometimes wish Mom went out, like Dara's mother. She doesn't have anyone but me and that can be a drag too. Like she's always going at me about things."

Dad was silent a moment. "Yes, I wish she would too."

"She's sort of bitter about men," I said. Maybe that was mean to say since Dad was the main man in Mom's life, but who can I talk to about it besides Dad? He's the only one who knows her as well as I do.

Dad was still looking thoughtful and slightly sad. "That can change," he said. "I certainly hope it will."

A conversation with Dad is really different from a conversation with Mom. With Dad I always feel there's some other thing right behind the thing he actually says that he would like to say or might say, but doesn't. I get the feeling it's hard for him to talk about personal things, but at the same time I get the feeling he wants to. I feel with him I'm kind of prodding him to reveal things Mom would reveal in one second. "How come you're not bitter about women?" I asked. "I mean, if she's bitter because you got divorced, you could be bitter too."

Dad smiled. "You ask really penetrating questions, Neens."

"You don't have to answer them."

"I want to. It's just . . . it's hard."

"Because I'm your child?"

"Yes, and because you're not really a child anymore—although you're not grown up, either. I don't like it when parents who are divorced force kids to take sides."

"You and Mom don't do that."

"Don't we? I'm glad."

"But how come you're not bitter?" I pursued.

Dad hesitated again. "Maybe because I have you. I mean, I have a person of the opposite sex in my life whom I love, and Jean doesn't."

That's interesting. I never thought of that.

"Also, I have Greg," Dad said. "We can talk about things. I think most people need someone to share their life with. Jean is very alone."

I thought of Dara's idea about the personals column. "I think she's pretty, though, don't you?" I said.

"Definitely."

"And she has a really good figure." Then I blushed. Imagine telling Dad that Mom has a great figure! As though he didn't know.

"There's no reason Jean shouldn't find someone," Dad said.

"And you, too?"

He looked startled. "Right. Me, too."

I stared off into space. "It's funny, though. I mean, I want you and Mom to be happy, but when I think of you both remarrying and maybe having new kids with those people, or marrying people who have kids already, whom I'll have to get along with even if I don't . . . then, I know this is selfish, but I almost hope you won't meet anyone."

Dad squeezed my feet affectionately. "That won't happen with me, hon. You don't have to worry."

I could have said, How do you know? Because obviously he doesn't know. Maybe tomorrow he could meet some divorcée with two sets of twins and fall madly in love with her. But I liked the feeling there was between us right at that moment, that we could get along and even discuss Mom in this calm way. It felt good; I smiled at him. "It's funny Mom giving up on men because of you," I said, "because whenever I compare any guy to you, they don't seem half as nice."

Dad smiled. I could tell he was pleased. "Well, that's the way you feel now."

"It's the way I'll always feel," I said heatedly. "I don't mean I'll never get married, but you'll never stop seeming nice."

Dad sighed. "I'm very lucky," he said. Then he stopped, like there was more he wanted to say but he'd decided not to. It had been such a satisfying conversation that I didn't even want it to go on longer. I didn't want anything to ruin it. I just yawned and said I felt like getting to sleep.

5

I won the election! I'm editor of *Info*. One thing happened that almost spoiled it. My English teacher, Mr. Gainer, really likes me. He thinks I have good ideas, and I always do my work on time. Even if I have to stay up all night to finish some book we have a test on, I do. Plus, I like him. He's a very friendly, unteacherish person, which may be because he used to be an artist and now is just teaching because he said he likes kids our age.

We had English the period before the election assembly, and at the end of class he said, "One of your classmates is running for a public office, and even though I know there's no electioneering at the polls, off the record I want to say if you don't vote for her, you're a jerk."

That made me feel terrible and wonderful at the

same time. I felt so good that Mr. Gainer wanted me to win, but a lot of kids hate teachers' pets. Also, it really isn't fair for a teacher to try and influence people. Frankly, I was afraid he might've just as much lost me votes as the other way around.

I took Dad's advice and took out the part in my speech about my only being a ninth grader. I tried to speak slowly. Once or twice my tongue kind of tangled around a word, but I just backed up and went slower. Luckily, I'm a little nearsighted so I didn't see people's faces too clearly. That expression, *a sea of faces*, is more what I saw, though I did notice Martina and Dara in the front row. In fact, having friends in the audience is just as bad, maybe worse, than people you don't know.

I was nervous listening to other people's speeches. The people running for *Info* went last and I was the very last person to talk. West Greenman, an eleventh grader, gave his whole speech in verse. It was really cute and funny. People laughed all the way through. I was sure he was going to win, but Dara said later maybe people just found him entertaining, and he didn't really try to convince people how he'd do a better job, the way I did. The other person, Carrie Rosen, wasn't very convincing at all.

We were in art class when the student-body president, Sandy Smith, called me out to the hall to tell me and congratulate me. When I came back in I was smiling. Martina, who has art class with me, was painting a landscape but dropped her brush and hugged me. Dara doesn't have art class with me; she takes dance instead. "That's so great!" Martina said.

"I hope I'll do a good job," I said. In a way it would have been easier not to win. What if people hand things in late, no matter what? I made it sound like I could solve a lot of things and make the paper more professional looking. Suddenly I wasn't sure I could.

"You'll be great," Martina said.

What do friends know? Obviously, they're not objective, but who cares. At times like this, you need someone just to give you confidence.

I'd promised Dara I'd go with her after school to Astor Place, where she has her hair cut. It's kind of noisy because a million teenagers go there. It's pretty rare to see anyone older—even Mom's age. Dara's always worn her hair short, but this time she said to the man who cut it, "Just whatever. You decide."

He held up her bangs, which were hanging in her eyes. "These—much too long. They must go."

"Okay." Boy, how can Dara be that calm? I always feel like I'm taking my life in my hands when I have my hair cut. I watched nervously as Pasquale trimmed her bangs and then shaved her hair really close on the sides. It was extreme, but it looked good on Dara, who has big black eyes that she makes up extremely skillfully. She wears eye makeup to school. She says it gives her confidence.

When he was done, he turned to me and said, "Next?"

"No, I'm just her friend," I stammered.

He went over and lifted up my hair. "You have enough hair for three girls," he said.

Dara laughed. "Yeah, but she's impossible. She'll never cut it."

I do have very thick hair and it is a pain at times, but I've just always worn it basically this way, below my shoulders and brushed to one side. "In summer you will boil," Pasquale said. "Let me give you a nice modern look."

"I don't have any money," I said, glad to have that as an excuse.

"I'll lend you some," Dara said excitedly. "It'll be to celebrate your getting the job of editor. You said you don't want to look young, like a ninth grader. Take a chance!"

It did seem dumb to have had the same hairstyle for my whole life. "Okay," I said. I looked pleadingly at Pasquale. "Nothing too extreme."

"Do I do too extreme?" he said to Dara.

"No, never," Dara said to me. She went over to where I'd been, on the window sill, while I edged into his chair. "He does it to suit the person."

Sitting there, I felt ten times more nervous than when I'd given the speech in assembly. Hair began falling in huge clumps to the floor. Pasquale seemed cheerful. He whistled and talked to other people while he was cutting. I wished he'd just shut up and concentrate on me. Then he turned the chair around so I couldn't see myself in the mirror. I heard this buzzing sound. "Please, not *too* short," I begged.

"It's going to look super," Dara said. "Wow, what a difference!"

Ten minutes later, I stared at myself in horror. I had no hair! Well, I had almost no hair on the sides, and just a big bunch of brown curls down the middle of my head. Somehow, cutting my hair had made it turn really curly. Dara must have sensed how I felt. "You have to get used to it," she tried to reassure me. "You look a million times older. Much more sophisticated. And you're so lucky! You have a natural curl now."

"You really like it? Dara, tell me honestly. You really think I look better?"

"Tons better. It's like you're a new person."

Even though I'd asked Dara to give me an objective opinion, I knew she couldn't. She wears her hair this way, so obviously she likes the style. The trouble is, I think it sort of types you. There are preppy kids at our school who wear jeans and neat shirts tucked in, girls and boys alike, and then there are the girls with their makeup and their Benetton sweaters. Those are the ones who flirt with boys non-stop all during school and boast about going up on weekends to prep schools or having older boyfriends out of school. Dara's look is associated with the group who are more punk. They dress the way I do, in wrinkly overalls and weird earrings shaped like skeletons or chandeliers. They're trying to be distinctive without looking like they spend tons of money on how they look. Most of their clothes they buy off the street or from Canal Jeans, where you get good values. I've always had more friends in Dara's group than any other, but I took a kind of pride in not looking exactly like them. Now I felt like a clone.

"Neens, don't worry," Dara said as she left me on the subway. "It'll take a while to get used to it. You had to do it eventually. You couldn't have worn it that old-fashioned way forever.''

"Why not?" I don't see why I couldn't have, basically. Going home I noticed a few people staring at me on the subway, giving me those intent, irritated glances people often give teenagers, as though they expected me to whip out a radio and start blaring rock music at them. Now it looks like I have a sign hanging around my neck, "I Am a Teenager," whereas before, who knows, people might've thought I was older.

Now I realized it was horribly unfortunate that I'd had my hair cut one of the days I was at Mom's, especially the day I'd won the election. I was sure she'd spend more time ranting about the hairstyle than complimenting me on winning the election. I wished I had a wig just like my old hairstyle so I could put it on as soon as I came home.

Mom left me a sign on the refrigerator: "Put hot dogs in the oven. Top with sauerkraut. Re-do salad dressing. Love, Mom." I looked to see if we had any dessert. We didn't, so in addition to doing the things Mom mentioned, I whipped up a bunch of brownies from a mix. I set the table perfectly; I even folded the napkins in a special way. All the while my stomach was in knots. Except for a quick glance at myself as I came in, I avoided looking into mirrors. I almost had the feeling that if I could forget about it being cut and think of myself as looking the way I had before, so would everyone, including Mom.

When Mom came home, I was sitting on the couch, leafing through *Seventeen*, looking for recipes to make for Dad for his birthday. "Hi," I chirped. I felt like a boy whose voice was changing. My voice kind of squeaked.

"Hi, sweetie," Mom said. "Umm, something smells good."

"I made some brownies. We haven't had them in such a long time."

"Super, I'm starved." Mom came into the dining room. She looked at me, but didn't say anything, didn't even seem to have any reaction. "When do you want to eat?"

"Any time's okay with me." I knew I was acting sickeningly servile, but anything to get her mind on other topics.

When we sat down to dinner, I said, "I won the election as editor of *Info* today."

"Great," Mom said. "I was praying you would."

I guess she didn't mean that literally because Mom's not that religious. "I worked a lot on my speech with Dad. I think that's what made the difference, since not that many kids knew me."

Mom looked hurt. "Why didn't you work on it with me?"

Whoops. I should never have said that. "Well, just since he's an editor, I thought he might be able to give me some tips."

Mom could have gone off the deep end about that, but instead she said, "That's true. I just wish Duncan would go for a better job. He's wasted on that little medical newsletter. He's a lot more talented than that."

"Maybe he likes it," I suggested.

"He does up to a point," Mom said, "but he's like me, he gets in a niche and he just stays in it because it's comfortable. He isn't that ambitious. We're alike that way." She looked sad.

"I hope I can do a good job," I said. "It's a big responsibility."

"You will," Mom said. "Just don't neglect your schoolwork."

That got me irritated. Mom always says things like that, like she has to deflate me just when I'm feeling good. "I don't neglect my schoolwork," I said sharply. "I'm just not a genius in everything."

"You don't have to be a genius to get a C in chemistry," Mom said.

"You yourself said you failed geometry," I pointed out. "How is this different?"

"I was going through a tough year at school," Mom said. "I mean, not with schoolwork, but I had just started going out with Duncan. I had a lot on my mind besides my studies."

"So does everyone."

Mom looked up at me intently. "Anyway, my point is: Do *better* than me, and better than Duncan, too. Don't just remake our mistakes."

"I won't," I said hastily. We'd been sitting at the table for a while and Mom still hadn't made any comment on my hairdo. I wasn't sure what that meant. Maybe she liked it! I definitely wasn't going to call her attention to it, but I was relieved we were just having what for us was a normal conversation.

Then when I got up to clear the table and go into the kitchen, Mom followed me. A minute later she let out a scream. "Oh, my God, your hair!" she said, as though I'd been in an accident and had both legs cut off. "What happened to it?"

"I had it cut." My heart was thumping a mile a minute.

Mom put her hands on the sides of my head. "You have no hair left! You're bald!"

"Mom, I'm not *bald*. Look in front. I have *plenty* of hair." I touched the topknot of curls, hoping they hadn't disappeared.

"You look like a *convict*," Mom said, her face horrified. "And you had such beautiful hair. Now you look like ... You know what you look like? One of those hard-core runaway kids they write up in the paper who's on drugs and steals things. Is *that* what you want to be? Is *that* the idea?"

"No," I said, really hurt. "Look, maybe it wasn't a great idea. I just wanted a change and Dara said she'd pay for it."

"Dara!" That got Mom going in another direction. "I knew it. Look at the home she comes from! A promiscuous mother in this day and age—"

"Her mother isn't promiscuous. She just has a lot of boyfriends," I said. "She really likes all of them." Dara says her mother claims "promiscuous" is just a word people use who are jealous that she can attract men so easily and they can't.

"She never knows where her daughter is. . . . You yourself said Dara ordered a green wig from a catalog because she wants attention. Obviously she's not getting enough at home. What's next? Prepare me."

I carried the brownies into the dining room. "Mom, listen, you sat through all of dinner and you didn't even notice my hair. So obviously it's not that noticeable."

"Wrong!" Mom yelled. "I'm just so self-absorbed and zonked when I get home from work, you could sit there with your head on the table in a *platter* and I wouldn't notice. You try working every day at a place where your boss is making out in the back room with his secretary and the caliber of men's consciousness is a negative number. If I couldn't tune all that out, I'd be a basket case!"

I was silent. "It'll grow in. . . . And it's good for earrings."

"If Dara comes here, I am really giving her a piece of my mind," Mom said, biting into her brownie. "*She* looks weird so she wants you to look weird."

"Mom, I wasn't copying Dara. She's really popular in our class. She's not regarded as weird except by really uptight, obnoxious kids who don't know any better."

"Your father said, 'Send her to a public school,' and this is the result: Every passing fad that sweeps along you give in to."

"Did you ever look at private-school kids? They wear their hair the exact same way."

Mom continued to eat her brownie. "Look, it's your life. Wreck it if you like. You're the one who will suffer in the end. I'll just suffer indirectly."

"Great." I stood up. "This was a great congratulatory dinner for my winning the election." With that I rushed to my room.

I know this sounds childish, but I cried. I felt terrible. The fact is, I do look awful. Dara is beautiful and she could shave all her hair off and no one would notice, or it might even start some new trend. I have a long nose and chubby cheeks. When I stopped crying, I stared at myself in the mirror. I looked like the ugliest person on earth, like one of those strange animals at the zoo that people laugh at the minute they see it.

They'll probably hold the election again when they see me. If I'd looked this way when I ran, I would have gotten minus two votes at best. Mom was right. I hated to admit it. Now I was worried about what Dad would say.

6

School the next day was the worst in my life. I tried tying a scarf around my head, but that looked even more idiotic than my hair. Finally I just walked in and sat down.

Damian Weil, who's on the *Info* staff, came over to me before classes started. "Congratulations about the election," he said. "I think you'll be excellent. Your essays in English are interesting. I was glad a ninth grader got it."

"Thanks," I said.

"I wanted to talk to you about an article I want to write." Then he stopped. "What happened to your hair?"

I tried to joke. "It got caught in a lawn mower."

"You had such nice hair," he said sadly.

Why are people so rude? Don't they know how

the other person will feel? They should at least lie, or try to. "Let's talk about your article some other time," I said, and walked away.

In English class we all were supposed to study while Mr. Gainer called each of us up for a private conference about our papers. The assignment was to write a poem from the point of view of a famous person. I picked Georgia O'Keeffe because I like her paintings. Instead of talking about my poem, Mr. Gainer handed the paper to me. I looked down. It had an A-plus written on one side.

"I wouldn't have expected it of you, Nina," he said severely.

I thought he meant my getting an A-plus. "Why not?"

"Because you have a mind of your own. What possessed you?"

"To do what?" I knew by then he meant my hair, but I decided to try and act cool and unconcerned.

He tapped his head. "It's ridiculous. It doesn't suit you at all."

"Thanks. I guess you wish you hadn't told people to vote for me, huh? Now you can make an announcement that everyone should take back their votes." My voice was trembling.

"I'm sure you'll do a fine job as editor. What's *inside* your head is superb. I wish the outside matched."

I felt as awful as I had with Mom, but I refused to back down. "Do you think you look so great with that beard?" I said. He just grew a beard this year, and it's about three different colors: red, brown, and gray.

"You look like some old hermit that's been living in a cave."

At that Mr. Gainer threw back his head and roared with laughter. "Just what my wife says." He reached forward and affectionately touched the tuft of curls in front. "I'm an old fogy. Who knows, in a day or so I might get used to it. I may even get one like it myself. How do you think I'd look as a punk?"

"Awful," I said. This is what I truly think: Adults who imitate kids look even dumber than kids do.

Throughout the day I felt like I was running a gauntlet. Everywhere I went people would call out "Sharp!" or "Hey, Nina, I love your hair!" I would say I got as many good comments as bad. It's just the bad ones sunk in more, maybe because I agreed with them.

Toward the end of the day I noticed Damian standing near my desk again. I glanced up at him sort of hostilely. "I never got around to telling you my idea for the article," he said warily.

"Yes?" I looked at him the same way.

"I'd like to write an article on gay students in our high school," he said, "how they feel about it, whether they think it's a problem."

"I didn't think there were that many," I said. "And who says it's a problem?"

"We don't know how many because a lot of them are too self-conscious to let it be known," Damian said. "But I think—"

"Are you gay?" I asked. I realized that was none of my business, but his comment about my hair still rankled.

He turned red. "No, but a member of my family is."

I looked at him. I wondered which member, but I just said, "Sure, you can write it. I won't promise I'll print it unless it's good. I want to have high standards for the paper this year."

"I'm the best writer in the class," Damian said with an annoyed expression.

"Who says?"

"One of the best, anyway. You don't have to worry about its being good."

Later I thought how snotty and awful I'd been to Damian, but I hate kids who are intellectual snobs like that, thinking they're superior to everyone just because they get all A's.

After school Dara asked if I wanted to go shopping with her, but I said no. "I overheard these girls talking and they said how terrific you looked," Dara said. "One of them said she never would have even recognized you."

"Yeah, I'll bet." I felt mad at Dara, which is really passing the buck because I could just as well have said no, I didn't want my hair cut. Also, she did spend her own money, and her allowance isn't any bigger than mine. I know her motives were good.

At home I looked through the *Seventeen* recipes again for Dad's birthday dinner. I finally decided on glazed Rock Cornish hens with rice and pignoli nuts, a salad, and for dessert a chocolate-orange mousse. I better start saving my money because Dad's birthday is in a week.

"Mom, do you know anything about Rock Cornish hens?" I asked at dinner.

"What?" Mom said. She'd been sitting across from me with a spaced-out expression, which usually just means she's tired or had a hard day.

"Rock Cornish hens," I repeated.

"What are they?"

"They're like chickens, but better. I thought I'd cook Dad a special meal for his birthday."

"Not bad. . . . What am I getting? Boiled elephant hooves?" She laughed grimly.

"I haven't decided yet. Something very special too."

"Does Duncan have you doing all his laundry, too?" Mom said. "Polishing the silver? I don't want him turning you into a free maid."

"Mom, first of all, I never do any of the cooking. Either Greg cooks or we order take-out stuff. And we each do our own wash."

"Just watch out," Mom said, "because it can start with Rock Cornish hens and the next thing you know, you'll be slaving away on three-course meals every day after school."

"I want to have a few basic things I know how to cook," I said. "No one said anything about slaving."

"Men sense an opening and go for it," she insisted. "I know Duncan."

I shook my head. "I know him too. He's my father."

"I've known him since I was fourteen," Mom countered. "I know a lot of things about him you don't know."

"Like what?"

Mom drew her finger across her lips. "Nothing."

"Well, stop saying things like that. Dad never says anything bad about you."

"I'll bet."

"He doesn't! We just talked about you and he said nice things. He even wishes you had someone to talk to, you know, like a boyfriend."

Mom narrowed her eyes. "That's so typical! A woman on her own can't be happy? Is that the idea? She needs a man to make her life complete? Look, I tried that and all I got out of it was a lot of grief."

"And me," I said sarcastically.

"Right . . . and you." Mom looked at me sadly. "And are you glad you were born?"

What a question! "Of course I'm glad. . . . Do you think I wish I'd never been born?"

"I don't know."

My mother says such strange things sometimes. I just stared at her.

"I felt so proud of you—winning the election," she said. "I just worry about your handling all these things, shuttling from one home to another, taking on added responsibilities. Isn't it too much? Don't you need time to just relax and have fun?"

"I thought you were worried about my grades." Boy, talk about contradictory!

"I am," Mom admitted, "but I think the rest of life is important too. Even boys. Maybe there *are* some nice ones. You've just got to look."

I looked at her hopefully. "If you feel that way, why don't you?"

Mom was gazing off into space. "It's a lot harder

at my age, it really is.... You'll find out when you get there, and now with AIDS and everything else ..."

After dinner I began thinking about Mom's remark, which seemed to imply that a boyfriend wouldn't be a bad thing, even for her, if she could find one. It's true. She doesn't meet anyone at work and she comes home tired. Maybe taking an ad as Dara suggested wouldn't be a bad idea. I have to do it just right, word it so it attracts really nice guys. I called Dara and said I wanted her help. Her mother has answered ads, as well as placed them.

"Come on over tomorrow for dinner and we can talk about it with Mom," Dara said. "She might have some good ideas."

I went in and asked Mom if it was okay if I had dinner at Dara's the following day after school. She said yes.

7

Dara's mother, Madge, used to want to be a ballet dancer, but she stopped growing when she was sixteen. She's only five feet two, and evidently ballet dancers have to be tall. She has a quite large bust and dancers are supposed to be thin and more or less flat on top. It's ironic because here I am, tall and flat, and I can't dance at all; I'm a real klutz.

"We ought to trade bodies," I told her at dinner.

"Oh, now I like what I have." Madge grinned. "In fact I like it a whole lot, but back then, when I was the age of you two, I tried to wear clothes so no one would notice. I was so self-conscious! I felt like I had these two *growths* hanging there, like tumors."

Dara is big on top too, and I've noticed sometimes, if we're talking to boys, they'll just start staring right at her breasts. Maybe they can't help themselves, but it seems rude. I'd mind, but Dara says she doesn't.

"I think this is nice of you, Nina," Madge said to me. "I wish my daughter had thought of something like this for me when I needed it."

"You!" Dara gave a hoot. "When did you ever need it? You've always had boyfriends."

"Not true," Madge shot back. "Remember when Perry moved out? I was distraught. I could hardly move."

Dara guffawed. "Yeah, sure, for one week, maybe."

"Dar, I'm telling you, I was devastated. That man got under my skin. It took me *years* to get over him. I mean *really* over. To this day I think about him."

"Why?" Dara looked at me. "He was this one-hundred-percent jerk. He wasn't even handsome!"

"He was incredibly sexy," Madge said dreamily. "That's something you can't tell just by looking at someone. He was really special in that area."

"Well, I never went to bed with him, so I guess I don't know," Dara said with a quick grin at me.

If I spoke to my mom like that, I'd be killed. Madge just said, "No, you *don't* know. So I'm telling you." She turned to me. "I think it's important to phrase these ads just right. You want to attract the right kind of person."

"Definitely," I said. "I don't want her to end up with some creep."

Madge got up and got a piece of paper and a pencil. "Okay, well, what're her interests? Let's start with that."

I thought. "She used to like going to the ballet. She doesn't go so much anymore. She likes old musicals."

"*Interested in the arts,*" Madge wrote. "How about sports? Tennis? Ice skating? A lot of men go for that."

"I think she went ice skating as a child," I said.

"How about more recently?"

"Gardening? Is that a sport?"

"Not exactly, but we can say *loves nature and the outdoors.*" Madge scribbled on her pad.

"Mom, that makes it sound like she's some Sierra Club nut like you," Dara put in. "It's not accurate."

"Hon, this is just general. If we make it too specific, we won't get any takers. Men are in a buyer's market—that's a fact." She turned to me again. "How would you describe her looks?"

It's hard to describe someone you see almost every day. "Well, she has blondish-brown hair and brown eyes and—"

"No, I mean more what's her general quality? Perky? Outgoing?"

I sighed. "Shy, basically."

"But she can get talking when she wants," Dara said. "*And* she's got a beautiful figure, Mom. Really. Nina saw her in the bath once."

Madge gazed off into space, biting the end of her pencil. "Hmm . . . Okay, how's this. *Shy but sensual young mother, interested in the arts, loves nature, is looking for that special someone for friendship and, possibly, romance. Let's get to know each other first. Please send a letter and a recent photo to . . .* Where? Your real address?"

"Maybe it's better if it's to a box number," I said. "Because I'm at my dad's sometimes and I don't want her to open them before I screen them out. Do you think a photo is necessary? I think she cares more about personality."

"Yeah, Mom," Dara put in. "Look at some of the guys you've gone with." She rolled her eyes.

"Like who?" Madge demanded.

"That Trevor whatever-his-name-was."

"Oh, but he was such a brilliant, witty man," Madge said, her eyes wide. "I never even noticed his weight."

Dara looked over at me. "This guy was, like, three hundred pounds."

"It was glandular, hon. He couldn't help it."

"I just think Nina's mom might be a little more particular."

"Okay, so that's why we're saying *send a photo*. That way Nina can get a rough idea if it looks like someone her mother would like."

I thought of the few dates my mother has been on in the past few years. "She's really fussy," I said, sighing.

"There's such a thing as being *too* fussy," Madge said. "If you start looking at everyone under a microscope, that's the end."

"Well, she can't change her mother's personality," Dara said.

"I know that," Madge said. "I'm a mother myself." She handed me what she'd written. "What do you think?"

"I think it's good." I began getting excited. I knew I shouldn't. If it was a buyer's market for men, as Madge had just said, would that many men be interested in a shy young mother? "Thanks," I added.

I went with Dara to her room. It's about the same size as mine, but the furniture is all new and matches. There's a Sierra Club poster on the wall and various rock stars Dara likes. As I lay down on Dara's bed, I realized Madge hadn't even said anything about my hairdo. Of course, she has different tastes from my mom, but still it was a relief. "It would be a whole lot easier if my parents had just stayed together," I said. "Then I wouldn't have to worry about them all the time, who they'll end up with, what their lives will be like once I'm grown up."

Dara was lying on the floor, her hands under her head. "Yeah, but Mom says that maybe I'm learning more about the way life really is than kids whose parents stay together and are happy. I'm learning that even if you pick the wrong person, life goes on, someone else comes along. I might make mistakes, but I know I can go on from there."

"I don't want to make mistakes," I said, suddenly frightened.

"You have to," Dara said calmly. "You live and you learn, right?"

"Sure, but to go through that whole thing, marrying someone, falling in love with them, even having a child with them and then . . . I don't know. I just hope divorce doesn't happen to me." My mood had shifted so fast it was scary. Sitting around the table before I'd felt good; it had seemed like a lark, planning Mom's possible future.

"Me, too," Dara said. "I hope my whole life is perfect in every way. I'm just not counting on it."

I think that's a good attitude.

8

I was able to place the ad for Mom over the phone. The lady at the newspaper gave me a box number and told me where I could pick up the answers. Maybe there'll be no answers! This sounds dumb, after spending the money for the ad, but I almost hope there won't be. If Madge went on a bunch of not-so-great dates, I bet it wouldn't bother her a bit, but with Mom it would bother her a lot. More than a lot.

When I went to Dad's, Greg was there and Dad wasn't in, so it seemed like a perfect time to discuss Dad's birthday dinner. It was that Saturday. Greg studied the recipes I'd brought. "Okay, no problem. Do you want me to do the shopping with you, or should I just draw up a list?"

"I can do it," I said. "Only can we, like, hide the

Rock Cornish hens? Because if Dad sees them, it'll spoil the surprise."

"Oh, Duncan never looks in the refrigerator. But I can wedge them toward the back." Greg began rummaging around. "We have pignoli nuts and rice. Let's see about semisweet chocolate." He got on a stool to look in the top of the cupboard.

"How're we going to do it so he doesn't see?"

"I can give you tips on how to do it, and then get him out for the afternoon. Or you can just say he's not allowed in the kitchen," Greg said. "It's up to you."

"Which do you think he'd prefer?"

"I think you could just tell him it's a surprise." Greg was writing things down on a list.

"Was Myra a good cook?" I asked.

"Who?"

"Myra, that woman you used to—"

"Terrible. . . . It's strange, here food is the most important thing in my life, and I'm always ending up with people who'd just as soon swallow a big vitamin pill." He laughed.

"Mom's afraid if I learn, whoever I marry will force me to do it every night," I said.

Greg handed me the list. "Nonsense," he said. "Everyone should learn. Food is life."

I went to the supermarket on Columbus Avenue, because Greg said he thought they have the best values in meat and fish. It's gigantic; it took me a long time to find all the various supplies I needed. I began pretending I was out of school, out of college and on my own, having some friends over for dinner. I imagined living in a nice apartment, and then I wondered: Will I be earning enough at whatever I end up doing to afford a nice apartment? Maybe I'll be sharing with someone. I think if I had to pick between Dara and Martina, I might pick Martina. It might be more relaxing living with her. I have the feeling Dara would want to go out every night.

In that way you'd think Mom and Dad would have been well suited. They're both sort of shy and don't like parties that much. Maybe they were too much alike. Dara, who's very outgoing, says she likes shy boys because it gives her a chance to draw them out. I think I'll be the opposite. I'd rather have someone draw me out.

I started remembering birthday parties when Mom and Dad were married. We never did all that much, but I always liked going out for some special meal. Even though neither of them liked to cook, they both liked eating out at special restaurants. Mom likes Japanese food; Dad likes Italian.

I got a little nervous when the woman at the checkout began ringing up my groceries. Greg had said to watch and make sure they didn't overcharge, but she did it so fast it was hard for me to tell. Luckily, I had just enough with a little change left over. It came to two fairly heavy packages, which they put in shopping bags.

When I got home Dad was already there, having a beer with Greg in the kitchen. I hate beer. I've tried it sometimes since Dad and Greg have it so often, but even the special, foreign fancy ones taste bitter to me.

Once Dara had a part in a school play where she had to get drunk and they made her drink a beer with no alcoholic content. She said it almost made her throw up, it was so vile.

"Neens," Dad said as I came staggering in. "All that stuff! You should have waited. I could have helped you."

"It's a surprise," I said nervously. "For your birthday. . . . Would you mind going into the living room while I put it away?"

Dad looked at Greg. "Hmm . . . Are you two in on something?"

"It's Nina's idea," Greg said with a grin. "I'm just the consultant."

They went into the living room. I unloaded all the stuff. Most of it wasn't perishable. The Rock Cornish hens I stuffed behind a big jar of dill pickles. I hope they don't just taste like chicken. I hope they taste special.

"Some friends of mine are giving me a party," Dad said when I came back into the living room.

"But mine's a party too," I said, alarmed. "It's for dinner."

"This is after dinner. I thought you might like to come."

"Will there be kids my age?"

"Maybe a few. I just thought you might like to meet my friends."

I was surprised. I didn't really know Dad had that many friends. He never seemed to before, when he was married to Mom. It might be fun going to a party with older people. "Sure, I'd like to come. Is it fancy? Do I have to wear a dress?"

"Wear whatever you like."

"What're you wearing?" Greg smiled at Dad.

"Who knows? I'll leave it to the inspiration of the moment."

Dad seemed in a relaxed, good mood. I wondered if I should tell him about the ad I'd placed for Mom in the personals section, but then it occurred to me that maybe, if it works, I could place one for him. Imagine fixing up both your parents with great people they never would have met otherwise! If I do that, it might be the first time someone my age did. I started wondering how I would describe Dad. Handsome? He is to me, but he's short and thin and his hair is beginning to shrink on top. Still, it's a buyer's market for men and I don't think women are as fussy as men when it comes to looks.

"That's some hairdo," Greg said, looking over at me. "You look a lot older, more sophisticated."

"Isn't that amazing?" Dad said. "I knew you looked different, but I didn't know what it was."

I touched my topknot self-consciously. I'd forgotten about my hairdo. Even though I just had it cut a week ago, I've almost gotten used to it. And I think maybe it's already grown in a little on the sides. "I thought you'd hate it," I said, smiling. "You're so square, usually."

"Me, square?" Dad laughed. "I thought I was as far out as they come."

"Look at the way you dress," I said. He had on a blue-and-white checked shirt and khaki slacks.

"Neens has a point," Greg agreed. "I think you need to liven up your image a little, now that you have such a sophisticated daughter."

"How about a green wig?" Dad said. "Do you think that's the answer?"

I laughed. Dad's about the last person on earth I can imagine in a green wig. I can better imagine Mr. Gainer in one. "My English teacher hated my hair," I said.

"Oh, what does he know?" Greg said.

"Is he that bearded guy?" Dad asked me.

Dad always goes to school conferences on a different day from Mom. I nodded. "I like him. In fact, he might have helped me win the election."

"No, not a chance," Dad said. "You won it by yourself. By giving such a good speech. Don't let Gainer try and take the credit."

"Do I look like an editor, though, this way?" I asked both of them.

Dad gazed at me thoughtfully. "Why not? Editors don't have to be guys with horn-rimmed glasses like me. If I'd had an editor like you, I'd have joined the school paper in a flash."

That night I lay in bed listening to Dad and Greg talk downstairs. I couldn't hear what they were saying, but it was comforting to go to bed with voices in the background. Sometimes at Mom's I wake up in the middle of the night and the apartment's so quiet I feel scared. I hate it if she goes to bed early before me. She always closes the door to her bedroom and sometimes I'll have this fantasy that someone's come in and murdered her, that she's lying there in all this blood, but I won't know until the morning when it's too late to do anything. I asked her once if she'd keep her bedroom door open, but she said she preferred it closed. I can understand that because I like sleeping with my door closed too. I didn't tell her why I'd asked. I don't really want her to know what a ghoulish imagination I have.

9

Dad's birthday dinner was a partial success. The big disappointment from my point of view was that, as far as I could tell, the Rock Cornish hens tasted exactly like chicken.

"Oh, no," Greg said as he bit into his. "It's a very different flavor—more subtle." He'd contributed a bottle of wine, which I thought was nice, because I didn't have enough money left.

"You're a gourmet," Dad said. "Neens and I are just plain old gourmands. We can't detect those subtleties." He turned to me. "But it's delicious, hon. Superb. You'll be putting this guy out of business soon." He smiled at Greg.

"I could take lessons from you," I said to Greg.

"Terrific. Just name a time," Greg said.

It's funny that even after spending all day cooking

or dealing with food, Greg doesn't get tired of it. I had a quick fantasy of running a restaurant, serving just the kinds of food I like, letting people sit as long as they want, keeping the tables far enough apart so it wouldn't be too noisy.

Dad ate everything and even asked for seconds. "You don't have to," I said as he held his plate out.

"I know," he said, "but I can't resist."

"Leave room for the dessert," Greg said. "It's the pièce de résistance."

From taking French I know that means something really special. "I hope," I added.

The dessert really was good. There was a slight orangy taste in the chocolate. Otherwise it tasted like extremely good chocolate pudding. "You really did all this yourself?" Dad said. "No help from any experts?" He looked over at Greg.

"I wasn't even allowed in the kitchen," Greg said. "I was just a consultant."

Dad pushed away his plate. "I am stuffed to the gills," he said. "And I bet Jimmy will have a ton of food."

"Who's Jimmy?" I asked. I felt pretty stuffed too.

"He's giving the party for Duncan," Greg said.

"Does he like to cook too?" I asked.

"Oh, occasionally," Dad said. "He's a doctor, so he works fairly long hours. But when he has time he cooks."

Greg gave Dad a bunch of country and western records, ones that are hard to get. I've never liked that kind of music that much, but Dad loves it and plays it all the time. He also got him some funny T-shirts. One was bright green with a black and white cow silk-screened on it. He also got Dad a bowler hat, a box of cigars, and a purple bow-tie. To my surprise, Dad wore all of those things to the party, except for the cigars, which he carried in his pocket.

"You look like a very eccentric businessman," Greg said.

I was wearing my red overalls and a white turtleneck with little turtles on it. The turtleneck might be a little babyish, but I like turtles. Greg wore a tuxedo jacket he said he'd inherited from his older brother, and a bright blue shirt.

"Did you ever wear the whole outfit?" Dad asked him when we were in the cab going down there; the party was in SoHo. "To a prom or anything?"

"Me? At a prom?" Greg made a face, horrified. "Can you picture it?"

"Why not?" Dad said. "Jean and I went to the senior prom. It was fun."

I tried to imagine that. Mom and Dad as teenagers, all dressed up, dancing cheek to cheek the way people did in that era. "Were you already going together?" I asked.

"We got married the next week," Dad said wryly.

"How did your parents feel?" I'd never asked Dad much about that time of his life because I was too little when they were together, and now that Dad's divorced he might feel funny about it.

"They thought we were too young." Dad looked out the window, more somberly. "Let's face it, we were."

"When I think of meeting someone in my class that I'd marry—" I said, "well, I just can't. Most of them are total creeps."

"Give them time," Greg said. "It just takes guys a lot longer to get their acts together. Sometimes I see some teenage kid who reminds me of myself at that age—kind of chubby and terribly eager to impress people, talking a mile a minute—and I feel like putting my hand on his shoulder and saying, 'Relax. You'll get there. Stop trying so hard.'"

I wonder if in twenty years that's how I'll feel about the way I am now, wishing I'd been more cool and sophisticated, more sure of myself. I looked over at Dad, but he was looking out the window with that same sad expression. I wondered what he was thinking.

Dad's friend Jimmy had a huge loft. He looked about Dad's age, in his thirties. He was wearing a regular dark suit. "Hi, Nina," he said. "I'm really glad to meet you. This guy never stops talking about you."

I smiled politely. I wonder if that's true. It made me feel good to think of it.

The party consisted of about twenty people, more men than women, but all of them about Dad's age. They all seemed to know who I was and everyone tried to act friendly. Still, it's hard being the only anything at a party, the only teenager or the only girl. The men were easier to talk to than boys my age, but I kept wondering if I seemed basically like a dumb little kid to them, or if I lived up to whatever Dad had said.

There was a punch that Dad said was alcoholic, but he added that I could try it if I wanted. I did. It was orangy tasting, with real strawberries floating on top. I've never been really drunk, but I don't think I want my first time to be when I'm with Dad and his friends. I might do something incredibly dumb—start singing silly songs or something. I went into the kitchen to get a glass because there weren't any more left. A really fat woman in a bright purple dress was leaning against the counter. Her name was Ethel; I'd been introduced to her earlier. She pointed a finger at me. I had the feeling she might be a little high. "I know where you got that haircut," she said.

"Where?"

"Pasquale at Astor Place," she said. "Right?"

I nodded. She had a big silver necklace on with little bells that tinkled slightly as she moved.

"How did you know?" asked a man in a white jacket.

"That woman at the gay parents meeting I mentioned. She goes there. She told him, 'Don't make it too extreme,' but he went right ahead. Whoosh! Now she looks almost bald." Ethel looked over at me. "You look super, hon. But when adults try to look like kids your age—"

"They look ridiculous," I finished up, together with her.

The man laughed. "I don't know. I never did any of those ridiculous things when I was younger. I feel like I want to do them now, before I get too old."

"Oh, sure," Ethel said. "At least I don't have to worry about that. I did more ridiculous things than you can think of. Just for shock value. Well, being gay in a small town in Kansas was no piece of cake, let me assure you."

"Tell me about it," the man said, smiling.

"They would have strung us from trees, if they could've." She let out a loud, bellowing laugh. "Only I'd have been too heavy to hoist." I listened for a while longer. It seemed a little strange that these were people who were friendly with Dad. Of course, he doesn't know all of my friends, either.

I found everyone was nice enough. Even though I'd see Dad across the room, I didn't go over to him. It's ironic that when I'm at parties with kids my own age, where I'd really like to make a good impression, I mostly feel almost sick to my stomach with anxiety and spend the whole time imagining it's over and I'm home in bed. If guys ask me to dance, I hate it because they want to press close to me and I usually hardly know them. But if no one asks me, that's worse. Here I guess the good thing was I didn't that much care. There was some music on but mostly people were eating and talking.

Toward the end of the party one man asked me if I wanted to dance. He was tall with curly brown hair and a T-shirt under which I could see he was really well built. "Hi, I'm Stein," he said. "I don't think we've met."

"I'm Duncan Calder's daughter," I said, "Nina."

He looked around. "The party boy? I don't know these people too well. I'm just in for the weekend. I'm a friend of Jimmy's. Do you feel like dancing?"

"I'm just in high school," I said. I thought he should know that.

Stein laughed. "So? You're probably a better dancer

than me. Be gentle." He reached for my hand. "How about it?"

"I'm not that great," I said cautiously. "In fact, I'm lousy."

"Worry not." We moved out into the room. Enough people were dancing so it wasn't like anyone would notice us. I think I did all right. Stein moved really well, not in a show-offy way, but just relaxed. Since I didn't have to worry if he liked me or would ask me out, I relaxed too.

After we'd danced a while, he went to get me another glass of punch, and got one for himself. I took a sip. I was really thirsty after dancing. "I'm afraid I might get drunk," I confessed. "I might even be already. I don't know how to tell."

"Do I have two heads?" Stein asked.

"No."

"Then you must be drunk, if you didn't even notice."

I laughed.

"If you were ten years older, I'd probably propose to you and we'd run off together next weekend," he said. "I'm like that. I'm the impulsive type. There's something innocent and cute about you."

Looking into his great blue eyes I felt excited and proud that he seemed to like me. "I'm not," I said, taking another sip of the punch. "The impulsive type, I mean. None of the boys in my class are that interesting. Some of them are good-looking from a physical point of view, but you can't talk to them about anything."

"Don't knock the physical," Stein said. "We're all

bodies deep down." He was sitting close to me and I suddenly felt self-conscious. I truly don't think my body is that great. Mom says it's just the self-consciousness of adolescence, but my breasts are mainly nipples and I have funny veins on my legs.

All of a sudden I looked up and Dad was standing there. "Hi," he said. "Having fun?"

"Yeah." I felt almost ashamed for Dad to see me flirting with someone, especially someone almost his age. "This is Stein."

"Hi, Stein," Dad said.

"Your daughter's quite a dancer," Stein said.

"She can do anything," Dad said in that proud, parental way that can be a drag though it's meant well.

"I'll bet." Stein winked at me in a way that made me feel funny.

I stood up. "Had enough?" Dad whispered. "It's almost one."

I leaned against him. He felt solid and warm. "Yeah, kind of. . . . I think I might be a little drunk."

I was afraid Dad would get mad, but he said, "Me, too. That punch was really lethal, wasn't it? I'm glad I stopped at two glasses."

"That's how much I had. Nice to have met you, Stein," I said rather formally since now Dad was watching.

We moved toward the door to get our coats. "Isn't Greg coming?" I asked.

"I think he wants to stay. I'll go speak to him a sec." I waited while Dad went across the room.

In the cab on the way home, I leaned sleepily

against Dad. I was afraid I might fall asleep before we got home.

"Did you have fun?" he asked quietly.

"Yeah, surprisingly."

"Why surprisingly?"

"Well, everyone was so old."

"Oh, right." He hesitated. "I hope that guy you were dancing with wasn't coming on to you."

"Stein? I don't think so. . . . But what if he was? What's wrong with that?"

"He's much too old for you, Neens. You didn't give him your phone number, did you?"

"No, but what if I had? Lots of girls my age go out. Maybe he thought I was mature for my age."

Dad was silent. "I'd hate to think it's that I'm jealous."

"Of what?"

"You're my little girl. I'm just not ready to, well, give you up to some other man. Or maybe he just didn't seem worthy of you."

"Hey, relax, Dad. He didn't ask for my phone number." I decided not to tell him that Stein had said if I were ten years older, he would've wanted to run off with me. Anyway, I had the feeling Stein was horsing around when he said that. I looked up at Dad. "I'd feel jealous if you had someone in your life too," I said. I knew it was because I had loosened up from the punch that I was saying that, plus his having brought it up in relation to me.

Dad looked worried. "Would you?"

"Yeah. I like it that I'm the main person in your life."

"What about Greg?"

"He's just your best friend. . . . I mean, you know—"

There was a long silence. Dad was looking out the window, then he looked back at me. "He's more than just a friend, Neens."

"What do you mean?" I said, knowing suddenly what he did mean.

Dad was looking extremely uncomfortable. "Maybe we better talk about this when we get home."

"Okay," I said.

For the rest of the ride neither of us said anything. All I could think of was: Let me be wrong. Let it not be what I think.

10

When we got back to Dad's apartment, I suddenly felt sick, like I might throw up. I knew I'd had too much to drink, but it hadn't affected me until then. I went into the bathroom and tried to throw up, but I couldn't. It was like there was a sick feeling right in the middle of my stomach that wouldn't go away.

Dad was sitting on the couch when I walked in, just the way he had when I practiced my speech. Before I even sat down I blurted out, "So what, it's like you're lovers?" I added quickly, "Like you're gay or what?"

Dad nodded. He looked miserable.

"How come you never told me? I feel like a jerk!"

"I was afraid." Suddenly Dad was next to me and reached out. "I don't want to lose you."

For some reason his being so nervous made me angry. I pushed him away. "You're a coward."

"In some ways, yes."

"You act like we're so close, you're jealous of my even having a boyfriend and then you ..." I was so mad, I couldn't even finish the sentence.

"I should have told you," Dad said. "I've been thinking of it for a long time, but I never ... There didn't seem to be the right moment."

"You're not even the type," I said. "You were married and all."

Dad took off his glasses and rubbed his eyes. "There is no type, really. And sure, some people know they're gay since they're your age. I didn't. Or maybe deep, deep down I had some feelings, but I tried to ignore them. I hoped they'd go away."

"Maybe they will."

"No, they won't, and I don't want them to. I love Greg and he loves me. That's been a ... revelation, even if it's painful in some ways. I just wish I hadn't wasted all those years denying it, being scared of who I really was—who I am."

I swallowed. My throat felt all tight, like I'd just eaten half a jar of peanut butter. "But if you'd known all along, you'd never have married Mom and I'd never have been born. So do you wish I'd never been born?" I felt like crying.

Dad had his arm around me. He squeezed me close. This time I didn't pull away. "Hon, you're the most precious thing in my life. Of course I don't wish that. ... And I loved Jean. It just—we couldn't make each other happy and neither of us really knew why. Now I know."

I was silent.

"How do you—how do you feel about it?" When he was little Dad had a stutter and it only comes back very rarely, when he's extremely nervous. I felt glad he was that nervous now. In a sadistic way I wanted to hurt him. I felt like he'd hurt me.

Somehow I pulled myself together enough to answer him.

"It's okay," I said coolly. "I mean, it's your life."

"It's your life too," Dad said. "Greg is going to move in. We want to start living together. We've actually planned for it to start tomorrow—after my birthday."

"Tomorrow? But you didn't even ask me! Were you going to do it without even telling me? What if I hadn't asked you that question tonight?" My voice came out shrill and squeaky.

"I was planning on telling you, either tonight or tomorrow morning. Actually that's why I took you to the party. To see some other gay adults."

"You mean it's just—it's all settled with Greg? What if I say no?"

Dad frowned. "Don't you think I have a right to love someone, to have my own life? What if I'd remarried?"

"You said you never would," I reminded him. "This is just as bad. It's worse!"

"How is it worse? You've told me that what worried you most would be my marrying a woman with kids or having a new family. This way you can be sure I won't. You'll still be the only Nina in my life."

Somehow that sounded *so* insincere. "This is so sneaky of you," I cried. "You tell me always to be open about things, and then you plan this for months and don't even *say* anything!" I looked at him accusingly. "Why?"

"Because of exactly what's happening. I was afraid you might have a volatile reaction. I was scared."

"What of?"

"That you'd back off, that it would disrupt the wonderful closeness we have together. That means so much to me. I don't want to spoil that. And you've always liked Greg. It won't be any different now."

I turned to him, trying to keep my voice down. "But don't you see? If Greg moves in, it *will* spoil things. He'll always be there. We'll never be able to talk the way we sometimes do. He doesn't know anything about kids! He never even had one. He probably hates them. Maybe he hates me!"

Dad smiled in a painful way. "Neens, how can you say that? Does Greg act like he hates you? Look how he helped you with my birthday dinner. He thinks you're wonderful. He's said a million times how lucky he thinks I am to have you."

"He's just saying that!" I said, exasperated. How could Dad be that naive? "Once he moves in, he'll probably act horrible to me."

"Well, if he does, he'll move right out again," Dad said.

I yawned. I felt sleepy and sick and angry, a miserable combination.

"Maybe we should sleep on this, Neens," Dad said. "I think because you're so tired maybe you are over-reacting."

"I'm not. . . . Nothing's going to be any different in the morning."

I thought of all the meals with Greg and Dad and me, both of them knowing but not telling me. I felt betrayed.

Dad put his arm on the couch, over me, but not on me. "There's one thing you haven't said anything about—my being gay."

"What should I say?"

"Whatever you feel. . . . Do you feel ashamed? Or—"

"No, I don't care about that. It's just I don't get why you have to go out of your way to be different. Maybe you and Mom just weren't a good combination. Maybe if you looked hard, you'd find a woman you'd like."

Dad hesitated. "Nina, the reason Jean and I didn't make it was *because* of this. I mean, sure, we have personality conflicts, but I think if this aspect of our life had been okay, maybe we could've stayed together."

I wanted to figure out some way to make this less awful. "Why can't we just go on the way we were? Till I go to college anyway? Greg can just visit you and, if you want, stay over when I'm not around."

"That's what we have *been* doing," Dad said, exasperated. "Neens, can't you understand this? I love you but, one, you're not here all the time and, two, I need another adult in my life. I need that security, that sense of connectedness. I want to share my life with another adult."

"So, are you going to get married to him?" I asked sarcastically.

"That particular aspect, going through a ceremony,

happens not to matter to me or to Greg. I've done that and it doesn't guarantee anything. For the sake of a child, I think it's worth it. Otherwise, it's just a piece of paper."

I leaned my head back. "Does Mom know?"

"I think she's sensed it. But we've never talked about it openly, if that's what you mean. Jean hates confrontation. Living by what other people think is much more important to her than it is to me."

That's funny because Dad seems so conventional in most ways. I'd have thought it was the other way around. "Are you going to tell her?"

"Eventually."

"Like when? When she's eighty?"

"No, sooner than that. I wanted you to know. I wanted you to understand. I feel like you can, and I don't know if Jean can."

In a way I felt flattered by Dad's thinking of me as more open-minded than Mom. "She'd probably go through the roof," I said. "If I were you, I wouldn't tell her . . . ever."

"That seems too underhanded," Dad said. "I think it might even be helpful for her to know, to realize the failure of our marriage wasn't anything she did wrong. I think deep down she still thinks that."

I thought of the personals ad. Before this I'd been hoping it would work, but suddenly the thought of both Mom and Dad having partners seemed scary. I'd be all alone. No matter what Dad says, he loves someone else now. I'm not that important to him anymore. That hurts. He's just trying to soft-pedal everything, pretending everything will be the same. It won't be. It can't.

Just then the door opened. It was Greg. He was still wearing his tuxedo jacket. He looked silly. Seeing Dad and me, his face got a guilty and nervous expression. I knew he wished I was asleep. "Hi, gang!" he said cheerfully. "Some party, huh?"

We both just looked at him. I guess he sensed what we'd been talking about because he said, "I'm kind of beat. I think I'll turn in. See you in the morning." He went to Dad's bedroom.

Somehow the thought of the whole thing, his sleeping over in Dad's bed, the two of them making love, however gay men do it, made me queasy. I wished so much Dad had decided never to tell me, or not until I was married or totally grown up. I looked at Dad. "You say he's so friendly!"

"Well, he's obviously uncomfortable. You're sitting there with a very hostile expression on your face. Greg isn't completely insensitive. He's been dreading this. He feels the way you do, that maybe we should just go on the way we were."

At least that was something Greg and I agreed about! "So, that's two against one," I said.

"That's not my style," Dad said. "My parents lived their whole lives like that, creeping around, scared of their own shadows. I've had to struggle with that since the day I was born. I don't want to live like that."

I stood up. "Okay, well, you've got it all set up so you'll be happy. I just have to like it or lump it, right?"

Dad looked pained. "You're acting just like Jean. . . . I never would have expected this. Do you enjoy making me suffer? If so, you're doing a great job. By the time you're twenty you'll be a real expert."

I was so hurt by his last remarks, I just walked away into my bedroom. I cried for half an hour. I kept thinking Dad would come in and apologize for saying that, but he didn't. He really meant it. He really thinks I'm like the worst parts of Mom. I can't think of anything in the world that would make me feel worse than that.

I hope he and Greg die in their sleep. I hope I come in and find them dead in the morning. That would serve them both right.

11

I slept heavily with all kinds of weird, awful dreams. One was that a murderer was loose, and Dara and Martina and I and some other kids from school were all hiding from him. But he found all the hiding places, and there wasn't any place left for me. I woke up in a panic, sweating.

The dream had seemed so real, I looked nervously around the room, as though the murderer might still be there. I was worried about something last night, I thought groggily. Failing chemistry? How'll I do as an editor? When I remembered, I felt sick all over again.

I showered and got dressed. When I came into the kitchen, Greg was making waffles. My dad wasn't up yet. Greg uses special whole-grain flour, and his waffles are usually pretty good. The waffle iron, which is ancient, was smoking. "I think it's ready," he said. "Feeling hungry?"

"Pretty much." In fact, I was starved.

I sat watching Greg pour the batter into the waffle iron. I was determined not to say anything about his moving in. I hoped he wouldn't either. He clamped the waffle iron shut.

"Did you have a good time at the party?" he said.

Everything about the way he was talking seemed false and stupid to me. "Yeah, it was great," I said sarcastically. "Especially the last part."

"I saw you dancing. You told me you didn't know how. You looked pretty good to me."

I just shrugged. I watched as Greg opened the waffle iron. Usually the waffle is brown and neat, with all the holes pressed down evenly. But this time it had split in half, and there were two burned-looking halves. "Ugh," I said.

"I guess I didn't add enough oil," Greg said. He began picking the burned pieces off, but they were stuck. He's such an expert cook, and he can't even make a waffle!

"I'm just going to have some cereal," I said. "That looks disgusting." I poured myself some Special K and milk, with a banana sliced on top.

"The next one'll be fine," Greg said.

"That's such an ugly old waffle iron," I said as I ate. "Why don't you at least get a new one, one that works?"

"I like this one. It belonged to my grandmother. Usually it works fine."

I chomped on my cereal while Greg picked the

rest of the two waffle halves off the iron, oiled it and started again. I hoped the next waffle would be just the same, burned and hideous-looking. But when he opened the iron, it was perfect.

"Look at that!" Greg said with a pleased smile. "A winner! Perfect! Sure you won't change your mind?"

If it had been anyone else, I'd have said sure because I love waffles, and at Mom's we never have them. My friends just buy frozen waffles. Greg is the only person I know who bothers to make them from scratch. But I just shook my head. I didn't want anything from Greg.

Dad walked into the kitchen. "Wow, that looks great," he said. "Who's it for?"

"You," Greg said. "You're the birthday boy." He slid the waffle on a plate and put it in front of Dad.

"That was yesterday," Dad said. "Right now I'm the furthest from my birthday of anyone here."

"Oh, don't be such a purist," Greg said. "Eat and enjoy. This is a birthday weekend. Two days of raucous celebration."

"Sounds great." Dad cut into his waffle. "Perfect," he said. "You know, it's funny, my mother made excellent waffles, and I just never could. They always stuck, or got burned, or broke in two." He snuck a quick, concerned look at me, as though trying to gauge if my mood had changed from last night.

"That's what the first one did," I said. "It looked terrible."

"There are those who would be daunted by one failure of such proportions," Greg said, "but not yours truly. *Ever onward* is my motto."

He and Dad sat there, eating waffle after waffle. If Dad doesn't watch it, he'll be as fat as Greg. I just sat there, watching them stuff themselves. "Maybe I'll have one," I said finally. My mouth was really watering.

"Neen, I wish you'd spoken up sooner," Greg said. "The batter's all gone."

"Can't you make some more?"

"Well, if you just want one, do you think it's really worth it?"

"Okay, I don't care. I'm not really hungry anyway."

Greg looked at Dad and then back at me. "I'm going over to get my stuff," he said. "It's all packed. I've hired a van. It won't be long."

I realized Dad was going over to help him. When Dad looked at me he still had that pleading, "will you forgive me" expression. "Want to come and help us?" he asked.

"No, I'm kind of tired," I said.

"Okay, well, see you in an hour or so."

After they left, I looked out the window. It was pouring rain out. I wondered if I should just go home to Mom's. I hated the idea of a whole weekend where I was supposed to act jolly and excited, like Greg's moving in was a terrific thing. I think Dad is really selfish. If I have children, I'm never going to make any major decisions that will affect them without asking their permission first. Selfish people shouldn't have children.

Before Dad's news, going back and forth between Mom's and Dad's was kind of interesting. I like being with Mom, but just as she was beginning to get on my nerves by flying off the handle over something minor,

I'd think, "Well, tomorrow I'll be at Dad's." But if Dad was acting quiet and removed and just poking around reading his medical magazines, I'd think, "Just two more days and I'll see Mom again." It seemed perfect now that I knew it was over. This way I'd spend all the time at Mom's dreading going to Dad's, having to have Greg around all the time, telling jokes, trying to be funny.

My dad is in love with another man, I thought. I just let that thought hang there and settle in. My mind raced. He's a freak, he's peculiar. He can't get along with women. He doesn't even like them that much. I'm a woman, or I'll be one some day. Maybe he won't like me. If Dad had spent all his life doing peculiar things, it would be different, but that's not what he's like. If only he hadn't met Greg! Maybe then he'd be like anyone else. Maybe then he'd have met some other woman, even.

I wondered how Greg and Dad had decided they liked each other that way. When I thought of them kissing or saying, "I love you," I felt so strange. Mom and Dad never did that publicly and I don't think people should. I hate it when kids who are going together in school make out in front of everyone. It seems so show-offy. Maybe now Dad and Greg will start acting like that, holding hands as they walk down the street, smooching.

I thought of their making love. Sex has always seemed not that appealing to me. I think I'd rather be a virgin all my life, and just have good friends. I don't even like boys to stare at my breasts when I'm *dressed!* The thought of anyone seeing me naked, and then lying on top of me, sticking his penis in me, seems awful. Some women bleed—the first time, anyway.

Knowing Dad and Greg wouldn't be back for a while, I broke down and called Dara. I just wanted to tell someone who would think about this news the way I do. Dara's the kind of person who, once she knows what you want her to feel, really backs you up.

"Something absolutely awful and disgusting has happened," I told her.

"What?" Dara asked excitedly.

"I can't even say it over the phone." I began doodling a picture of a lion.

"Is it something about a boy? Someone you like?"

"No!" Dara always thinks everything has to do with boys! "Except it makes me feel like I never want to have anything to do with them."

"Oh, you're always saying that," Dara said with a laugh. "Why won't you tell me? Now I'll spend all weekend worrying."

"I just can't," I said. That was true. Even though I'd called her up to tell her about it, I found I didn't want to say anything over the phone.

"Well, just give me a hint. What's it about?"

"My dad."

Dara laughed. "Oh, I know. He has a girlfriend, right? Look, that always happens eventually. You've just been lucky so far that neither of your—"

"That's not what it is," I cried, exasperated. "It's the opposite of that."

"The opposite of that is what's already been going on," Dara said, "that they don't have lovers. . . . Boy, you're making such a big deal out of this! Mom has had so many freaky, crazy boyfriends I can't even count them. I'm used to it. They need adult companionship, that's what she says. They need sex, let's face it, even at that age, although they better be careful now."

I was silent. If I didn't tell Dara what I was talking about, she couldn't be much comfort, but I still didn't feel like telling her. "You don't know what it is, so why don't you stop going on about your mom."

Dara was silent a minute. "Don't be such a bitch," she said. "I'm just trying to be sympathetic." Suddenly she sucked in her breath. "Oh, my God, I bet I know. It's something with your dad's friend, Greg. I bet he made a pass at you, right? Or he, like, tried to rape you?"

God, Dara thinks every problem in the *world* is about sex! "No!" I said. "You're as wrong as you could possibly be."

"Okay, well, just sit around and suffer, if that's what you want. . . . Are you going to tell me on Monday?"

"I think so." I hung up.

The rest of the weekend was boring and dumb. Greg and Dad spent most of the time trying to decide where to put Greg's furniture. They would ask me, "Do you think this looks nice here?" as though they were making this deliberate effort to include me. If you ask me, Dad has enough stuff already. Now the apartment looks too crowded, like some old furniture warehouse. Plus, Greg's taste is different from Dad's, so the things don't really go together. It was just like I'd told Dad it would be. They spent every second talking to each other, and I was like some unnecessary person who happened to be there, taking up space. I don't even know if I feel like coming over here every week if this is what it's going to be like.

12

Of all the bad timing, on Monday Damian handed me his article on someone in his family being gay. I read it in study period because I'd already done all my homework. It was about his older brother, and how his parents had reacted when he told them, and how he felt about it himself. I saw him watching me read it, which made me self-conscious. The minute study period was over, he rushed to me. "So, what'd you think?" he asked.

Damian is so conceited! I think he is a good writer, but I knew he expected me to say it was the greatest thing ever written. "It's okay," I said, enjoying watching him deflate in front of me.

"Just okay? What's wrong with it?"

"It just seems sort of superficial, like, big deal, my brother's gay, what's the problem."

"That was my point," he said. "That to my parents it *was* a problem. Whereas I just see it as a choice, or maybe as the way some people are born."

"You're really broad-minded," I said sarcastically.

Damian looked at me, puzzled. "Do you think it's better to be narrow-minded?"

"Let me read it again," I said. I knew I was acting supercilious and mean. "I couldn't concentrate that well."

"Okay." He looked cheerful. It felt good to have that kind of power over someone.

At lunch hour sometimes Dara and I skip out and just have an apple or some yogurt on the fire escape. The lunch room at our school is so noisy, and the food so putrid, you never miss much. We're not allowed to leave the school grounds for lunch. They tried that a few years ago, and supposedly too many kids never came back after lunch. To them that proved that kids our age can't handle responsibility. I wish they would make only the ones who didn't come back not be able to go out for lunch instead of punishing everyone. But they didn't ask us. Probably by the time we graduate they'll have gone back to the other way.

Dara says this way we're getting healthier food, bringing our own stuff; she's always dieting anyway. She'll probably turn *into* an apple, she eats them so much. "I saw Damian talking to you after study hall," she said. "I think he might like you. He never talks to anyone else."

"It was just about some article he's written for *Info*," I said, wanting to squelch her fantasies before they got out of hand.

"Is it any good?"

"It's fair," I said.

"I think he's very smart," she said. "I wouldn't mind it if he liked me."

"Dar, I just told you it had nothing to do with that! So relax!" I glared at her.

"In terms of pure looks, he might not be the best," she went on, as if I hadn't even said anything. "But his being so smart makes a difference."

"Do you want to hear what I called you about on Saturday or don't you?"

"Of course I do. What is it?"

I paused for dramatic effect. "My dad's gay. . . . He told me. And Greg, who you think is so sexy and terrific, is his lover."

"So, what's so terrible about that?" Dara said, munching on her apple.

"Well, how would you feel if your father—"

"My father's a total shit!" Dara cried. "He told me he never wants to see me again! Your father is nice. He treats you so well."

"He used to . . . Now it's like it's just the two of them together. I'm a real fifth wheel."

"That's what it's like in the beginning," Dara said, "when they're going through the lovey-dovey phase. You should have seen Mom with that guy Trevor. I almost got sick. You know how she's always saying there's nothing more valuable to a woman than her independence? Well, with him, if he'd said, 'I want you to crawl in here on your hands and knees with my slippers in your mouth,' she'd have done it. I mean it!"

"But at least she's normal," I said.

Dara looked at me incredulously. "Normal? Are you kidding? What's normal about her? *Your* mom is normal, mine is crazy."

"I thought you liked her."

"Sure, I like her. I'm used to her. But no one in their right mind would call her normal. Even *she* wouldn't call herself that."

I couldn't seem to explain it so she would understand how I felt. "It would be different if I'd had any idea, but Dad and Greg just acted like friends. Would you have guessed?"

"Not especially. . . . But maybe he was afraid that was how you'd feel so he kind of bent over backwards to make it look like they were just friends."

"Don't you think that's sneaky?"

Dara carefully wrapped her apple core in a napkin and put it in her purse. "I don't know. They need their privacy just like we need ours. I certainly would never tell Mom every time I made out with someone. She'd kill me if she knew about Don!"

Don's that older guy in Vermont. "I just wish he'd waited till I was in college," I said. "Then I'd be away from home."

"But that's three years away," Dara said. "By then he'll probably have broken up with Greg."

"Why?" I was horrified.

Dara shrugged. "I don't know. That's just the way it is."

"But Dad's not like that."

"How do you know? Who says Greg is even the first? He might've had dozens of lovers before him, only he made sure they were out of the house before you got there. Just make sure you don't go around kissing all of them."

"Why should I kiss them?" I looked at her like she was crazy.

"I'm just saying, be careful. You could get AIDS, or something."

"Dara, we studied AIDS in Ms. Roper's class. You don't get it from kissing. And I'm not worried about Dad and AIDS. I think Greg is the first one and I'll bet anything he and Dad will be just a regular couple now."

But just Dara's saying it did get me worried. I could accept Dad's being gay, maybe, if someone promised me he wouldn't go around risking his life by going to bed with lots of different people. I didn't think he would, but I decided I'd better ask him, just to be sure.

I thought of Dad's saying he wanted to share his life with another adult, to feel connected to him. "You don't think your mom will ever settle down?" I said.

"Oh, maybe, when she's really old, forty or fifty or what have you, when she can't get dates. She says then she's going to marry a rich old man and push his wheelchair around, someone who'll leave her a whole lot of dough when he kicks off." Dara grinned. "Which wouldn't be bad for me because then I could share it and we could travel together."

I wished Dara would take my problem more seriously. "So, the gay thing wouldn't bother you at all? What if it was your mom, for instance?"

Dara let out a hoot. "Boy, I'd love to see that! She's so man crazy. I'd love to see her be gay just for even two *seconds!* No woman would put up with her. Men think she's sexy."

"I guess one thing Greg and Dad have in common is that they both were married. Or at least Greg used to have that woman friend, Myra, he lived with."

"Yeah," Dara said. "So maybe it's just a phase. Mom has a friend like that. She swings both ways. AC/DC is what they call it."

Somehow it seemed to me like that would be even more confusing. I don't think I'd like that. I'd rather Dad was one thing or the other.

After school I went to pick up the letters that had come in from that personals ad. It had only been in for a week, so I wasn't sure there would be any replies. I was really surprised: There were six!

I waited till I got home to open them. Each man had written a one- or two-page letter. Some of them weren't that well written. I couldn't help reading them as an editor, the way I do with *Info* articles. One guy couldn't even spell, although he said he was an accountant. He spelled "extremely" with only one *e* and at the end he said, "hoping to be your special freind." I don't think Mom would like someone who can't spell. Not everyone sent photos either, which must mean they're really ugly because I said specifically that they should. One man, someone named Manuel Vasconi, wrote: "This is my college graduation photo. I've lost some hair since then, but I still look very much the same. My waist is still 34"." That must mean he's bald as a billiard ball. It's so easy to get into one of those quick photo places. And Mom'll see what he looks like when they meet, so who does he think he's kidding?

The one I liked best was a man who said he'd been married before, and was also shy. He said he had a thirteen-year-old daughter whom he was very fond of and who was "the emotional center of my life so far." Then he added something that sounded a little like what Dad had said. He wrote: "I can't say I'm lonely, my life is busy and full, but someday I would like to share it with someone. Tracy will be grown and gone in such a short time. I don't want to burden her with my emotional needs. Can you understand that?"

Basically, I thought they weren't bad. None of them sounded like jerks or mean people. Of course, they were trying to put their best foot forward. They could have horrible character traits they're just not mentioning. The only one I felt suspicious of was this lawyer who said sensuality was important to him also, and he thought without that as a base, no relationship would work. He hadn't even read the ad right! I just said, "Shy, sensual young mother." I didn't say she thought sensuality was important. She doesn't. I was just trying to hint that she had a good figure. I thought if I said, "has a great body," that would, for sure, attract sex maniacs. Mom may even hit the roof if she sees I put "sensual." Maybe I should've just said "sensitive." That's more accurate. I want to show all the letters to Dara before I decide which ones to show Mom. If she reads a wrong one first, she might not read on to the good, possible men, like the one with a daughter my age.

I started dinner for Mom: pork chops and baked sweet potatoes. She seemed sort of silent when she came home. "Did you have a good weekend?" I asked.

"Nothing to write home about," Mom said. "How was yours?"

I stared at the saltshaker. "Fair." My heart started thumping, I guess because of my having this secret about Dad that Mom didn't know about. But I didn't want to get her in an upset mood before her birthday. Dad said it might make her feel better to know the reason that they didn't make it as a couple wasn't her fault. I'm not sure. She could just get mad that he hadn't told her to begin with.

"How did your birthday dinner turn out?" she asked.

"Which one?"

"For Duncan. Weren't you going to cook him Rock Cornish hens?"

"Oh, right." For some reason I'd forgotten that whole part of the weekend. "It turned out well. Only they're pretty much like chickens. I don't get why they're supposed to be so special."

Mom just shrugged.

I kept looking over at her while we ate. Mom eats looking down at her food. There's something so discouraged and sad-looking about her when she eats, like some old dog poking around in his bowl. I wish Mom would get a more sexy hairdo, or maybe dress a little more colorfully. She looks like she almost wants no one to notice her.

After dinner, just as I got out of my bath, Mom called out, "Neen, phone!"

I wrapped myself in a towel and went into the bedroom. The other extension is in the kitchen. "Yeah?" I said.

"This is Damian Weil."

"I didn't have a chance to reread your article yet," I said quickly. "I will."

"Okay. . . . Uh, that wasn't what I called about."

There was a pause. Was I supposed to ask him what he *had* called about? I didn't.

"I called because I wondered if maybe you'd like to go to the movies this Saturday."

"With you?" The minute I said that, I realized how silly it sounded. Who else would he call about?

"Right. . . . Would you?"

"Which movie?"

"Any one. Is there any special one you'd like to see?"

If I said there was, that was practically agreeing to go. "I usually go to my father's from Thursday to Monday," I said.

"Where does he live?"

I told him Dad's address.

"Oh, great, that's right near me."

I swallowed. "He's kind of strict," I lied. "I don't know."

"I'll get you back before midnight," Damian said.

This was the first time in my life anyone had ever asked me out, so I hadn't had any practice. I knew you can't say, point blank, "I just don't feel like going out with you," but I decided to try to be reasonably honest. "I don't usually go out on dates," was how I put it.

"Well, this won't be a date, exactly," Damian said. "We'll just go to the movies."

Was that a promise that in the movies he wouldn't suddenly grab my hand or start feeling around in the dark to see what parts of me he could touch? Dara says boys are like octopuses in the movies. They wait till you're all absorbed in the movie and then, quick as a flash, they're all over you. I was too embarrassed to ask if that was what he meant.

"You go to the movies with your friends, don't you?" Damian said.

"Yeah."

"Well, this'll be like that. I just want to be your friend."

I felt like I'd run out of excuses. Anyway, if he tries anything, I can just remind him of what he said. If all he was interested in was making out, he could find lots of girls more willing than I am, and with better figures. Of course, he may have called half the girls in our class. I'll never know. "Okay," I said, trying to put some reluctance into my voice, so at least he wouldn't get the idea that this invitation was the most exciting thing that happened to me.

He asked if seven-thirty was all right, and I gave him Dad's exact address. It was just bad luck that it happened to be near where he lives. The luck of the draw, as Dara would say.

13

Thursday after school I usually go to Dad's, but somehow I just didn't feel like it. I knew deep, deep down why I didn't, but I couldn't face any of my feelings. They were too confused, I guess. I asked Dara if I could stay over at her house instead. I told her I wanted her advice on the personals letters.

When we got to her house, Madge was just coming in from tennis. "I showed the girls my tattoo," she said.

"Were they impressed?" Dara said, a little sarcastically, in that flip way she talks to her mother.

"Were they ever! Jill said it was like a painting. She said the man who did it was a real artist, and I said he really was."

"What tattoo?" I asked, curious.

"She got a tattoo on her—" Dara began, but Madge interrupted.

"I want to surprise Nina. Nina, come into the bedroom. I'll show you."

We went into her bedroom and lay on her big water bed while she disappeared into the bathroom. The shower started running. Dara looked at me and smiled. "She makes this into such a big production," she said. "Everyone who comes over here, she shows it to! She's probably going to show it to the doorman next."

"I never heard of a woman getting a tattoo," I whispered.

"Wait till you see where it is."

"Where?"

"You'll see in a sec."

A few minutes later Madge came out of the bathroom with a towel wrapped around her. "Close your eyes," she said.

I did.

"Now, open them."

I opened my eyes. Right in front of me was Madge's behind. There was a big sunflower tattooed right on one side. It had petals and leaves going out in all directions. It really was like a picture, it was so real looking. "That's pretty," I said, embarrassed. Usually you don't have a chance to stare at someone's behind that way. "How come you, uh, picked a sunflower?"

Madge turned around to look at it admiringly in the mirror. "My daddy used to call me Sunflower when I was little, Sunny for short because of my sunny personality, I guess. And I couldn't see having a dragon, though they *were* pretty."

"I never knew women had tattoos," I said. "I thought it was just sailors."

"Oh, lots do," Madge said. "You'd be surprised. Now when I see some person walking down the street, I wonder if they have one, and where it is."

I didn't want to seem rude, but I asked, "How did you think of that . . . place to put it?"

"Well, he said he needed a large working surface, and I didn't know it was going to work out so well. I wanted to wear a bikini without it showing, so I figured my butt was big enough and pretty flat—at this stage anyway." She laughed. "In another ten years it'll probably look like a sunflower that's been left out in the sun too long."

"I would *never* do a thing like that," Dara said emphatically.

"Well, no one's saying you should," Madge said. She hooked on her bra. "But I can tell you, I've had a lot of compliments. In fact, I've had nothing *but* compliments, even from the most straitlaced people, ones who, like you, might never have the daring and imagination to do it themselves. Sometimes I wish I could show it to everyone in the world!"

At that Dara looked over at me and we cracked up. We started giggling, and couldn't stop. Every time I'd begin to gather myself together and calm down, I'd think of Madge showing her sunflower to some completely unlikely person like Mr. Gainer when she went for a school conference.

"You two," Madge said, shaking her head. But she sounded relaxed.

Imagine my mom doing something like that! Not that I wish she would, but it does show you how different mothers can be. If I even told Mom about Madge having it done, she'd probably think it was so crazy, she wouldn't let me visit here anymore.

Madge fixed us a big salad for dinner with black wrinkly olives and feta cheese and tomatoes. Like Dara, she's always dieting. And like Dara, she never seems to lose any weight, but she goes right on doing it.

I told them I'd gotten six replies so far to the personals ad.

Madge looked pleased. "That shows we worded it just right. Any good ones?"

"I liked the one who also has a thirteen-year-old daughter," I said. "I figure they would have something to talk about."

Madge and Dara looked at each other. "Well, that doesn't count," Madge said.

"What do you mean?" I asked, spitting out an olive pit.

"Mom once had this boyfriend with a daughter my age," Dara said, "and it was the absolute *pits*. I mean, he'd bring her along on dates, and expect all of us to spend the evening together. If *he* stayed over, *she* stayed over."

"He had to do that, hon," Madge said. "She was just nine and he had full custody."

Dara was poking around in her salad. "Why didn't he get a baby-sitter?" Then she turned to me and said,

"Boy, what a drip! She was my age, but she acted like such a baby. Can you believe this? She still drank from a bottle! She claimed it made it easier to drink, like cocoa in bed, but that was just an excuse."

"Kids from divorced homes often have problems adjusting," Madge said. "You have to learn not to be so critical."

"*I* don't," Dara said. "Nina doesn't."

"You two are special," Madge said. "Divorce makes some kids more mature, others less." She got up to clear the table. "I think that would be terrific, Nina, having a man who's a father. At least that way he understands how complicated it all is. And those men are less likely to be out just for what they can get."

"I thought you said he was only interested in having someone to clean house for him," Dara said.

"*He* was," Madge said. "What was his name? I can't remember."

"You're the one who had an affair with him," Dara said. She gave me a slice of melon with a scoop of vanilla ice cream on top.

"It's just flown from my mind," Madge said. "Premature senility, I guess."

"If you didn't do it with so many people, maybe you could remember them," Dara said, with a grin at me.

Madge was cutting the skin off her melon. "Well, Miss Smarty-Pants, if you saw how many men I've turned down, you might sing a different tune. They would fill Madison Square Garden."

"And the ones you *didn't* turn down would fill

up Carnegie Hall!" Dara said with a snort. We both started laughing.

I really wanted to eat dessert, but every time I looked at Dara, I'd go off again. I tried to think of serious things, but nothing worked. Madge just sat there, eating her melon. "Talk about babies!" she said.

We went into the living room to read the letters. Madge read them aloud. I guess I was just in a silly mood, or maybe it was Dara's influence, but all the letters sounded hilarious. Even Madge started laughing. "Oh, no, listen to this one," she said.

"Sensuality is important to me, too. Without it a relationship cannot work. Love without sensuality is like an ice cream soda without fizz, like the Fourth of July without firecrackers, like a beautiful woman with big feet—"

"He should see your feet," Dara said. "He'd run for the hills."

Madge was laughing, but she held up her hand. "Let me finish, will you?

"I don't want to be unduly modest, so I can tell you honestly, that my ex-wife says her years with me were the happiest of her life—"

"How come she's his ex-wife, then?" Dara interrupted.

"My sister says that when she looked for a husband, her role model was me, her baby brother.

Even my mother admits that I have never disappointed her or let her down, never failed to send her flowers on Mother's Day.

"Who's he going to bring in next, his ten cousins and his eight aunts?" Madge said as she set down the letter. "See what I mean? Buyer's market. This guy probably looks like a dog's dinner that's been left in the sun for two days, and he thinks the sun wouldn't rise in the morning without him. I've had more dealings with those than I care to remember."

They both liked the man with the daughter named Tracy. "He does sound sincere," Madge said. "Count him in. . . . Plus, she's a teenager, and it doesn't sound like he necessarily has full custody, so he wouldn't drag her along on dates."

"Keep your fingers crossed," Dara said. She was chewing gum, which she says helps her to concentrate. Most of our teachers don't let you chew gum in class, which is why, Dara complains, her grades aren't good. She says she won't go to any college unless it says "Gum chewing allowed in class" in its brochure.

Of the six letters, Madge put the man with the daughter in the A category, she put two others in the B category, and two more in the C category, which she said I should keep as reserves if the first three didn't work out. The man who thought he was God's gift to women she put aside. "That one deserves framing, for all the times I forget about the size and dimensions of the male ego," she said.

Just then the phone rang. Madge answered it. "It's for you," she said.

It was Mom. "Where are you?" she said, her voice shaking.

"You *know* where I am! You just called here."

"You're supposed to be at your father's. He called, all upset, saying you never came home after school. We were beside ourselves."

"I'm sorry," I said. "I forgot."

"Well, will you call him this *second*?" Mom said. "And Nina, please, never, ever do that again. You're supposed to be responsible about this. You know that."

"I said I was sorry," I repeated. When I hung up, I turned to Dara and said, "I need to make a call in the other room."

"Sure." She pointed to her mother's bedroom where the phone is.

I sat on the edge of the bed for a while, wishing I didn't have to call Dad. I wish Mom could've called him for me, telling him I was spending the weekend at Dara's. He answered the phone. "Hi, Dad? It's me."

"Nina! Where are you? Greg and I were extremely worried."

Right away I got annoyed. Greg was probably happy at the idea that I'd been mugged—maybe killed. If Dad can fall for that, he'll fall for anything. "I'm spending the weekend at Dara's," I said. "I meant to call you, but I forgot."

"Any special reason?"

"No. There're some things we've been planning to do."

"You're sure that's all? It doesn't have anything to do with what happened last weekend?"

"I'm sure."

Dad hesitated. "If you change your mind—I mean, if you decide you want a change of scene, we'll be here. Just give a call. I'm here for you."

I wish, in a way, I never had to go to Dad's again. That would serve him right. I didn't want to think about it, but I found myself pouring out to Dara how I felt. Dara was used to strong feelings, I guess. She had an idea I'd never considered. "Why don't you not stay there anymore?" she said. "Would your mom mind if you moved in full time?"

"Why should she mind?" I asked.

"Mothers like their privacy," Dara said. She was painting her toenails.

"Mom doesn't go out," I reminded her. "She's all alone when I'm not there. She'd probably be glad."

"That was in the past," Dara reminded me. "After she starts dating some of the people you've picked out for her, who knows, she may never be home."

Even though I hoped my plan would succeed, that sounded a little unlikely. "My dad would mind, though."

"So, he should have thought of that before moving this guy in," Dara said.

I looked at her purplish-pink toenails. I'd never paint mine, but if I did, I would definitely not pick a color that looks like soggy watermelon. "You said you thought the gay thing didn't matter."

"He can sleep with whoever he wants, although he should be careful, but moving them in—that's another story. That's where I draw the line. I told Mom:

She can date any fool on earth as long as I don't have to live with him."

"I thought they slept over sometimes," I said, "your mom's dates."

"Sure, an occasional sleep-over is one thing. But a total move in—no way! He should've at least asked you how you'd feel about it."

I laughed grimly. "He knew I'd say no, I suppose."

"So, fuck him," Dara said.

"Right." But it was hard for me to feel that way quite as easily as Dara might. She hates her dad, pure and simple, whereas I don't hate mine. I just wish things were the way they were before. Maybe I was too smug, thinking things would never change. But even if I hadn't been, I wouldn't ever have expected this.

14

Saturday, Dara and I decided to go to the Village. Her mom gave her her allowance, and in the morning we sold a bunch of her old records on the street and made another thirty dollars. Dara said I could share it, which I thought was extremely generous.

We went to a bathing suit place near Eighth Street. All I wanted was a tank suit, a plain old regular suit, and can you believe, in a store that said in the window they had five thousand styles (though that might have been an exaggeration), every single one was cut way up on the side, or had some strange cut-out in the front, or a neckline that plunged down to your belly button. "These are all terrible," I said. I looked at Dara, who was in a purple suit with a red and yellow tie to one side.

"I think this one is really cute," she said, admiring herself in the three-way mirror. "It makes my legs look long, and I think it makes me look really thin. . . . What d'you think?"

Personally, I don't think anything makes anyone look thinner than they really are. Dara still looked like a busty short person with not-that-long legs. "I don't think I'm going to get anything," I said, discouraged.

"The blue one looks cute," Dara said.

"But it's cut so low," I exclaimed. "I don't want people gawking at me all the time."

Dara looked surprised. "But that's the whole point of a bathing suit! Would you want to walk down the beach and pass a bunch of really cute boys, and have them not even notice you were there?"

"Yes!"

"Boy, you're weird." She bought the purple suit and a white bikini. If she thinks she looks thin in the bikini, she needs glasses. You can see how her stomach comes out in front. "Mom says men like fuller, womanly figures," Dara said.

It shows what a good friend I am that I didn't even answer that.

When we got home, Dara modeled the suits for her mother. "Cute," Madge said.

Dara pointed at me. "She wouldn't get any. She said they were all too revealing."

"I don't know," Madge said. "Ever since I went to France where on some beaches even ladies in their fifties and sixties went around with nothing on, I don't see the point of suits at all. The human body is beautiful. Why hide it?"

"Not all bodies are beautiful," Dara said, patting

her bottom. "Some are ugly. . . ." She looked at me. "What if some guy was talking to you and he got an erection? That would be so embarrassing! I'd die."

"So would he, probably," I said. I knew what she meant. If they ever have beaches like that over here, I'll definitely never go to one.

"Why would you die?" Madge said. "It's perfectly natural. It just shows someone is attracted to you."

Dara made a face. "Ugh, imagine having some penis pointing right out at you."

"I know!" I said.

"What don't you like?" Madge asked. "That it happens, or seeing it?"

"Both!" we said together.

"Well, you're still young." Madge laughed. "You'll see a lot of them, eventually."

Not me. I hope I see one, at the very most. When we went back to Dara's room I said, "I wish people didn't even have bodies. It would be a lot easier."

"I guess you get used to it," Dara said. "Like with anything."

I'm not so sure. Otherwise why would there be so many unmarried people? Maybe they never got used to it. I may end up one of those.

Dara seemed pleased with her purchases. Before she put them away she took out all her clothes and went through them, deciding to give some things away. "You can have first pick," she said.

I tried on some of the things she was discarding. There was a bunch of T-shirts that looked like they'd be good for the summer. "I grew out of those," Dara said proudly, like having big tits was some kind of accomplishment.

"They'll fit me fine," I said. She was giving away some ugly bell-bottoms and a corduroy skirt she said her mother had made her buy.

"Want those?"

"You've got to be kidding. . . . I'd take your denim jacket, if you don't want it."

Dara looked at me in horror. "That's my most prized possession."

I knew it was. I was just teasing her. I can't believe how neat Dara is. Her closet has everything stacked up in piles, according to colors. I just hurl things in and hope Mom won't check. I've forgotten I had some things just because they fell down in back of my closet and sort of disappeared.

We looked in the TV guide. There was a James Dean movie playing at eight. "Oh, great," Dara said. "I love him. He's so cute. Did you ever see him?"

I shook my head yes.

"Let's watch that first and then maybe the special on teenage pregnancy. That should be really interesting."

"Why? What's so interesting about teenage pregnancy?"

Dara was holding another pair of jeans up in front of her. "Well, someday it could be us, if we're not careful."

"It could not! . . . It could never be me, anyway."

"Aren't you even going to go out with guys?"

"No, why should I?"

Just as I said that, I remembered I was actually supposed to be on a date with Damian. He was supposed to meet me at Dad's house at eight o'clock! "Oh, no," I said. I started toward the phone, but before I even got there, it started ringing. I picked it up.

It was Dad. "Could I speak to Nina, please?" he asked.

"Dad, it's me. Is Damian there?" I felt uncomfortable, first because of not wanting to see Dad, and then because of Damian.

"I believe that's who it is," Dad said. "An attractive young man in a blue shirt and jeans?"

"Listen, this is awful, but I forgot. So much has been going on I forgot, that's all. I had a date with him."

"Well, should I tell him to go home and forget about it? He seems to be under the impression that you were going to see a movie."

All the time we were talking, Dara, who'd followed me in, was pawing at me, saying, "What? What?"

I put my hand over the receiver. "Shut up. I can't hear anything."

"Tell me what it is!"

I felt even more embarrassed. "I was supposed to go to the movies with Damian and he's at Dad's house. I completely forgot."

Dara rolled her eyes. "Boy, that is so typical of you. You never even told me."

"I forgot, I just said. What should I do? He's over there right now!" Of all places. How dumb. I felt panicked.

"Say you'll go over in fifteen minutes. You're not going to get all dressed up, are you?"

"I don't even feel like going, for lots of reasons," I mumbled.

Dara brightened up. "Well, listen, I'll go. How about that? *I* think he's nice. He's not exactly my type, but—"

Meanwhile Dad was saying, "Nina? Are you still there?"

I spoke quietly into the receiver. "Tell him I'll be over in fifteen minutes. Don't, um, tell him I forgot. Just say I was doing something and it got later than I realized."

"Okay," Dad said. "See you soon."

When I hung up, I made a face. "How stupid! Why'd I say yes, and then forget?"

"You forgot because you don't want to go," Dara said calmly. "Come on, let me take your place. At least then he'd be with someone who'll *try* to have a good time."

"He didn't ask *you*," I snarled.

Dara looked at me. I was wearing jeans and an old ratty-looking gray shirt. "Are you going to change?"

"Into what?"

"I'll lend you something. . . . How about my purple top and my denim jacket?"

"That purple is so bright." I wasn't sure. I didn't want it to seem like I'd gone out of my way to look that different from the way I look at school.

"Suit yourself. Look in the closet." Dara lay back on her bed. She seemed to be getting some kind of satisfaction out of my predicament.

I knew I didn't have much time, so I finally picked a green top, pretty much like the purple one but not as loud.

"How about makeup?" Dara said.

"I don't wear any."

She dragged me into the bathroom. "Oh, come on. You're such a party pooper. Why'd he even ask you out? He must be a masochist."

"Thanks a lot."

Dara was examining my face. "I like you, but . . . well, maybe he likes challenges." She blobbed some foundation on my face and rubbed it in and then drew pink lipstick on my lips. When she started going at me with her mascara, I yelped. "No! That's enough. Leave me alone."

"Okay, calm down." She looked at me through narrowed eyes. Then she walked me to the door. "You look nice. Have fun. Oh, and listen, wake me up the second you come back, even if it's, like, three in the morning."

"It won't be. I'll be back while you're watching that stupid special on teenage pregnancy."

She grinned. "And you'll be out doing it!"

"Wash your mouth out with soap, you jerk!"

Why do I put up with Dara? She has a filthy mind, and she's boy crazy. Sometimes I wonder what we have in common. But hurrying over to Dad's, I felt bad. I thought about my conversation with Dad. I thought about forgetting a lot of things I didn't want to think about. Mom and Dad have been going at me for not being responsible enough. Once at Mom's I forgot to take my key out of the door so when she returned home it was just sticking out. Anyone could've taken it, robbed our apartment, and murdered both of us in our sleep.

I knew my forgetting this time was a combination

of not wanting to go on the date and not wanting to go to Dad's. But I was glad I hadn't backed out and let Dara go in my place. I'd hate thinking of myself as a total coward. Poor Damian might be insulted.

15

When I got there, Dad and Greg and Damian were sitting around, talking and drinking beer. Maybe if I hadn't come, they just could've sat around all night going on about some ice hockey team they all watch on TV.

Damian looked up and smiled as I came in. "Hi, Nina!" he said, as though I wasn't forty-five minutes late.

"Want a beer?" Greg asked.

"No!" I turned to Damian. "I'm really sorry."

"That's okay. There's something that starts at nine-thirty: *Smooth Talk*."

"I've heard that's good," Dad said. "It's about teenagers, from a Joyce Carol Oates short story."

Damian stood up in front of Dad. "I might get

Nina home a bit after midnight, sir ... if you don't mind."

Imagine Damian calling him sir! "Whenever," Dad said.

"I'm sleeping at Dara's," I said, embarrassed. "We have this project that we're working on for school."

"Oh, okay." Damian looked a little puzzled. I felt embarrassed.

Once we were out of the apartment, I felt better. We hurried along to the movie. It was close enough to walk, about ten blocks.

"Your father and his friend seem really nice," Damian said.

"Well," I muttered. "It may seem that way."

He looked at me in surprise. "Aren't they?"

"I don't want to talk about it, okay?" I snapped.

"Sure. ... Did you have some kind of fight? Is that why you weren't there when I arrived?"

"I said I didn't want to talk about it!"

"Oh ... all right."

We walked on in silence. I realized I should be making some kind of conversation, but I didn't know what to say. "How come you called him sir?"

"What should I have called him?"

"It just sounded so weirdly formal."

"That's the way I was brought up," Damian said apologetically. "My father's kind of strict about stuff like that. Maybe that's why, when my brother told them—"

"Yeah, I remember," I said quickly.

We got to the theater on time. *Smooth Talk* was okay, though I certainly would have felt more relaxed if I'd been watching it with Dara. It was the story of a really pretty girl who's supposedly fifteen, but looked more like twenty-two. She's always flirting with guys and making out, but then runs away. At the end, some older guy she hardly knows follows her home when her parents aren't there and makes her go away with him in his car. I was scared he might murder her, but he didn't. He might've raped her, though. I wasn't sure. They just showed a field, with the car parked nearby. If I had been with Dara I would've just asked her, "What do you think happened?" and we would have discussed it. It's my own fault. If I'd met Damian on time, we could've seen some other movie that was about animals or something simple.

I felt so embarrassed watching the scenes where the heroine makes out with some boy she meets at a shopping mall and then runs away. And I felt really scared at the end, when the awful man comes in his car to force her to go away with him. That's like a lot of my nightmares. Damian didn't try to hold hands with me, or put his arm around me. I sat very straight, and once or twice our shoulders touched, but that can happen with anyone.

"That was a strange movie," he said when we got out. "I'm not sure I understood the ending."

"Me neither. . . . At least he didn't kill her! I was afraid he was going to."

"He might've done something even worse," Damian said.

I couldn't figure out what that meant. What could be worse than someone killing you? Anything would be better than that because then you could at least go on to do other things. "What do you mean?" I asked. "What's worse than being killed?"

Damian looked really embarrassed. "Well, I thought he might've . . . when they showed that field, I thought maybe he made her—"

"Yeah, but would that be worse than being killed?" I broke in because I was afraid he'd never finish the sentence and, besides, I didn't want him to.

He still had a nervous expression. "For a girl, maybe," he said.

My mind was racing. I don't think anyone in the world dreads sex more than I do, but I think it can't be *that* bad. I laughed nervously and said, "I guess I don't know."

What a stupid thing for me to say! Did I think he thought I *did* know? That I'd been raped once? Or that I'd been raped and killed, and thought being raped was better? I wished I'd thought to bring Dara on the date with me.

Damian said, "Let's go in that coffee shop and have some ice cream, okay? I'm hungry."

I supposed it would be rude to say no. "My dad likes me to get home before midnight," I said. It was eleven-twenty.

"I thought you were staying at Dara's," Damian said.

"Oh, right, I forgot. Usually I stay at my dad's."

We went to a place nearby. We sat down in a booth and ordered ice cream sodas. This made it seem more like a real date. Before, it was more like just going to the movies. "That girl was really pretty," Damian said thoughtfully.

"Who?"

"That girl in the movie."

"Yeah, only she looked so old! How could they say she was fifteen? She looked like she was twenty-five." I sucked up the soda from the bottom of my glass.

"Some girls look like that pretty early," Damian said. "My sister did. Even when she was that age."

"Did what?"

He looked embarrassed again. "She, you know . . . looked older."

I guess he meant having a good figure, which didn't make sense because the girl in the movie didn't have that much on top, even. Dara has more. I started thinking of Dara and me trying on bathing suits and my decision to not buy one. I looked up at Damian. He was poking at his soda with his straw.

"Before," he said awkwardly, "when you didn't come, I thought maybe you were standing me up."

I turned red. "No, I just . . . It was something different." Standing someone up sounds worse than forgetting, though maybe it amounts to the same thing.

"It's just you didn't sound that eager on the phone." He looked right at me with his hazel eyes.

I hate it when people put me on the spot. What could I say? "I don't go out on dates that much," I admitted. "In fact, this is the first one I ever went on."

"Me, too," Damian said. "Some guys in our class are onto their fifth girlfriends! At camp, at other schools. You'd be amazed."

I bet he'd be amazed if he knew about Dara fooling around with a twenty-two-year-old guy. "Girls, too."

He grinned. "Maybe we're just late bloomers."

I, personally, don't think thirteen is late. I think I may be a never bloomer. "I'm not in a hurry," I said, just to make sure he didn't think I was desperate to get started.

"I don't see the point in going out with just *any-one*," Damian said. "It's a waste of money. If it's not someone I can talk with about things, I'd rather stay home with a good book."

"Me, too." I wondered if I wouldn't rather be home with a good book right that second. Or even watching that stupid teenage pregnancy documentary with Dara. I thought of her dumb remark, "and you'll be out doing it." If Dara was a boy, I'd never go out with her in a million years. Sometimes I don't understand how we can be good friends so much of the time.

"I think you're doing a good job as editor," he said. "I'm thinking of becoming a journalist when I graduate from college. Do you want to be one too?"

"I haven't really planned it out yet," I said. "My dad's an editor of a medical newsletter. That's how I got interested in this."

"You write well," he said. "Do you think I do?"

"Yeah, I do. But I think you're like me, you write better when it's about a topic, about facts. I hate it when Gainer makes us write something personal, about our life. I never know what to say!"

Damian hesitated. "That article I gave you, the

one about my brother being gay, that's probably the most personal thing I've ever written. Did you think it was terrible?"

I realized now that I'd just read it quickly and put it aside. That was before I'd found out about Dad and Greg, but I wondered if just seeing the article had made me nervous. Now, looking back, it seems like I knew more than I was willing to admit I did. "I have to go back and read it again," I said, "but I think it's a good topic. A lot of people might be ashamed or just uncomfortable acknowledging what you wrote about."

"I was," Damian admitted. "But then I thought maybe there'd be other kids in the same situation or a situation like it and this might help them."

There was a pause. I wondered if Damian had picked up that Dad and Greg were gay just in that short time he'd spent with them. Even if he had, I had the feeling he was too polite to say anything about it. I could have told him, but somehow I just couldn't. "I guess we should be getting back," I said, feeling awkward.

Damian took me back to Dara's apartment house. For a second I was afraid he might lean over and kiss me. There was something about his expression that gave me the feeling he was thinking about it. But at the last minute he reached out and shook my hand. "Thank you for a very enjoyable evening," he said, and turned away.

It was twelve-thirty when I walked in. I prayed Dara was asleep. She was, but the TV was still going and the lights were on in her room. I turned the TV off, but when I turned off the light, she woke up. "Neen?"

"Yeah?" I started taking off my clothes.

Suddenly Dara was wide awake. She turned the light on again. "So, how was it? What'd you do?"

"We went to a movie, *Smooth Talk.* . . . It was strange."

"I saw it with Mom. Wasn't Treat Williams sexy?"

"Who was he?"

"The man at the end who takes her away in his car."

"Sexy? He was horrible!" I yanked the T-shirt off my head. "I didn't even understand what happened. I thought he was going to kill her, but then she came back. Did he rape her or something?"

Dara yawned. "No! He just made love to her. He broke her in, kind of . . . I wouldn't mind it if someone like that broke *me* in."

"Dara, she didn't even *know* him! Remember how she got all hysterical and was crying? She was scared out of her mind."

"So? I'm just saying *I* wouldn't have been . . . She was probably like you, just the fact that he was sexy made her go off the deep end."

"You mean you'd want a totally strange man you didn't even know who talked in that weird way to *force* you to go off with him? What if he had killed her?"

"But he didn't! He said he only wanted to be her friend . . . Anyway, if she really didn't want to go off with him, why didn't she call her folks or something?"

I just can't believe sometimes how crazy Dara is. "She was scared. She couldn't even dial the phone, her hands were shaking so much!"

"Oh, anyone can dial a phone," Dara said with a snort. "She really wanted him. She was just playing hard to get."

"You are crazy," I said. "I mean it."

"Maybe you are," Dara shot back. "Anyhow, how was the date? Did you, uh—"

"No," I yelled.

"Nothing? Not even in the movies?"

I shook my head.

"You probably brought a pin to stick him with if he tried anything." She laughed.

"I didn't. We just watched the movie."

"Well, I guess he doesn't like you that way. Maybe he just wants to be your friend. When Tommy Cole told me that, I cried my eyes out for ten days. Then I figured: So? I'm not his type. That's not my problem."

I was getting into my pajamas. "Not all boys are sex maniacs," I said. "Maybe he just has good manners."

"Didn't he even kiss you good night?"

"No."

"Or maybe he's just weird." She grinned. "Then again, maybe he needs someone a little more experienced to show him how."

"Like who?" I asked sarcastically, knowing she meant herself. I turned the light off again.

"The special on teenage pregnancy was really good," Dara said in the dark. "I learned a lot of interesting things."

"Tell me in the morning," I said sleepily.

Dara went on, as though I hadn't said that. "Did you know there's only one day every month someone can get pregnant? Maybe even less. Maybe just twelve hours."

I just yawned. "Umm," I said.

"And did you know . . ."

I don't know how long she went on, but I fell asleep in the middle.

16

When I saw Mom again Monday evening, I said, "Mom, how would it be if I stayed here with you all the time?"

She looked surprised. "You mean, not go to Duncan's at all?"

I nodded.

"Is something wrong? Did anything happen?"

"No," I said slowly. "I just . . . I don't know. I think I like it better being here with you. But if you feel you need your privacy or something . . ."

"I'd love having you here, sweetie. I'm really touched. I thought we weren't getting along that well these days. I always had the feeling you were closer to Duncan."

I shook my head.

"He's going to be very disappointed," she said. "What are you going to tell him?"

"Just that I have a lot of work with school and being editor and all. It might not be permanent."

"Okay," Mom said. "But just make sure you put it nicely, and don't give him the impression this is something I foisted on you. He's very sensitive about that."

I almost wished Mom had put up more of a fight. Now I just had to call Dad and tell him. That seemed the hardest part. I put off calling him. I didn't feel like going into the thing about Greg's moving in. He knows how I feel about that. Finally, I called him and told him what I'd told Mom, that I had a lot of schoolwork and I thought it was easier for me. Since Mom lives much closer to my school, I could get home more easily if I had to stay after school for meetings.

Dad listened in total silence. "Have you spoken to Jean about what we talked about?"

"No."

"I just want to be sure she isn't putting pressure on you in some way. Do you swear to me she isn't?"

"Yeah, it's my idea. I never told her about what happened."

Again Dad hesitated. "You know how badly I feel, Neens. Can you talk to me about it? I suppose that's the point. You're trying to punish me."

"No! It's exactly what I told you."

"What if Greg moves out? Would you reconsider?"

I got excited at the thought of that. But if I said yes, that would make it seem as though that was the only reason. "Then you'll just move someone else in," I replied.

"No, I certainly wouldn't do that," Dad said. "I love Greg. Whether he lives here or not won't change that. But if you find our relationship hard to accept—"

"No, it's fine. I don't care," I said. I really didn't even want to talk about it. "I need some time and that's that."

Again there was a pause. "Please think it over," Dad said. "Maybe I didn't handle this right. But if I were to lose you, it would be a terrible blow. You know that, don't you?"

"Yeah, kind of."

He laughed. "Kind of! Well, I hope we'll at least talk on the phone from time to time. It's hard for me to call you. I don't like to get Jean. But any time you want to call me, do . . . And if you change your mind and want to go back to the old schedule, let's just do it. No excuses necessary."

"They're not excuses!" I said. "I've got to go."

I hung up, feeling terrible. I tried to think: if I was God, or He could appear and ask me exactly what I wanted, what would I ask for? I think I'd ask for everything to be the way it was before. I didn't mind Greg coming over to Dad's *sometimes*, especially when he cooked good meals. I wouldn't mind if Dad and Greg were best friends, like me and Dara. I just wish they didn't have to be gay. And I wish they didn't have to live together. Or it could have happened once I was away at college. Then, who cares? Home'll just be a place to come back to on vacations.

At least Dad didn't fly off the handle and say I *had* to stay with him, the way Mom would've if I'd said I didn't want to stay with her anymore. He took it the way he takes everything, seemingly calmly, though he did manage to get in that dig about "excuses." Excuses are just a way of being polite. He should know that. I was mad at Dad—he was right—but I didn't want to punish him. There he was wrong.

That weekend was Mom's birthday. Sunday morning seemed like a perfect time to leave her the personals letters on her plate. I was planning on making her waffles, too, from a regular batter recipe we had. If Greg can do it, I can. I know Mom likes waffles because she always orders them the times we eat breakfast out.

Saturday she asked me if I'd gotten a bathing suit the day I'd gone shopping with Dara. I shook my head. "I couldn't find any I liked," I said.

"Well, why don't we go together this afternoon? I need one too. There's a place in the Village that says in the window they have five thousand styles."

"That's the place Dara and I went to," I said, wrinkling my nose. "They were all terrible."

"Five thousand terrible ones? In what way?"

"I can't explain. Just fancy or ugly."

"Well, with five thousand styles, we're bound to find *something* we like. Maybe you didn't look in the right places."

I knew we'd looked everywhere, but since her mind was set, I had to agree. "I think just a simple tank type is best," Mom said. "Unless you want a bikini. I know a lot of kids like those."

I looked at her in horror. "No, absolutely not!"

"We'll find some tank suits, then," Mom said.

We went that afternoon. She marched into the store and began going through all the styles in sizes that would fit us. I'm an eight and she's a ten. "There is nothing on God's earth more depressing than shopping for a bathing suit," Mom said pensively. "I think they're designed by sadists who've never seen a woman's body." She began picking. "These all have some strange aspect to them. . . . Well, these are the closest to tank suits they have, I guess." We wedged our way into the dressing room. It was really small. Both of us began getting into the suits. I snuck a look at Mom's figure, thinking of the ad. "Shy, sensual young mother . . ." But then I felt embarrassed. I pray Mom thinks the ad was a good idea.

Mom was in the purple suit Dara had ended up buying, only Dara's a size twelve. She stared at herself in the three-way mirror, frowning. "Look at the way this is cut!" she said. "It's absurd. It's cut halfway up my legs and down to my belly button in the front."

I'd gotten into a brown one. "Mine is too."

"This is awful." Mom marched out of the dressing room and right up to the sales desk. Someone else was buying some suits. "Look at these suits!" she said.

The woman who was ringing up the other purchases said, "I'm busy with a customer right now. Gwen! Can you help these ladies, please?"

A girl who looked like she was just in her teens

came over. "What seems to be the problem, ma'am?" she asked.

Mom pointed to the suits.

"What's wrong?" the girl said. "I think they look great."

"My point," Mom said, fuming, "is, that with all your presumed five thousand styles, don't you have just a plain, ordinary tank suit, something my daughter and I won't be ashamed to be seen in?"

"That's just what you're wearing," the woman said. "What do you call that?"

My mother pointed at the one I was wearing. "Look at the way this is cut! You can see her breasts as clear as day. She's only thirteen!"

By now I was really mortified. If only Mom didn't make such a big production out of things.

"They develop early these days," the other woman said. "That's not my department. I think she looks cute as can be."

Mom dragged me back into the dressing room. "What a terrible woman!" she hissed. "I'm never shopping here again."

"Me neither," I said. "Let's just forget about it. I can swim in my shorts and T-shirts."

Mom was pulling on her panty hose. "Certainly not. We both need suits, and I cannot believe that in this entire city there is no store that has a simple tank style. We'll find it if it takes us all day."

The thought of that made me exhausted and depressed. "I don't even like to swim," I said.

It didn't do any good. We spent the next four hours marching up and down Broadway, replaying the same scene. In the last place the store manager was a man. He smiled at Mom as he said, "Honey, if I had your figure, I wouldn't wear a suit at all. I'd just go around as nature made me."

Mom turned bright red. She hates those kind of guys. "Let's go home," she said to me. "I can't take any more of this."

In the cab on the way home I said, "He just meant you had a good figure, that man in the store."

"I know what he meant," Mom snapped. "I've been around men a lot longer than you have. Well, we just won't swim there. It's their fault. They're losing sales. There are probably thousands of women just like us who'll be forced to stay off the beach all summer, simply because of pig-headed salesmen, or insane swimsuit manufacturers."

"Right." I was beginning to feel rotten. I'd wanted Mom to be in a good mood for opening her letters.

I tried to get her into a better mood by offering to treat her to dinner. I'd saved up my allowance, since I hadn't bought any clothes last weekend. Mom seemed really pleased. She dressed up, as though we were going on a date. She chose a seafood place on Columbus, since lobster is her favorite dish and she never makes it at home. "I haven't got the heart to throw them in boiling water," she said, though she does have the heart to eat them. She had a glass of wine and said I could, if I wanted. I said I'd rather have a soda.

"This is fun," Mom said, "doing things together like this." She was picking away at her lobster, looking happy.

I wondered if she'd included shopping for the bathing suits as fun. "I used to hate going shopping with my mother," Mom said, "because she had such strong tastes. She always bought things for me that *she* wanted, not that *I* wanted. But I think our taste is quite a lot the same, don't you?"

"In some things," I said diplomatically.

Mom sipped her wine. Maybe she should have wine more often. It makes her kind of mellow. "Actually I do like your friend, Dara," she said, "but if I were her mother, I'd worry about the way she dresses. Boys can get the wrong idea so easily."

For some reason, I guess because we were getting along, I told Mom about my date with Damian. "He's a really good writer. He writes articles for *Info* sometimes."

"As long as you don't feel you have to get involved with him, against your will," Mom said.

"Of course not!" Before you know it, I get annoyed with Mom. She assumes I'm a total bowl of jelly as far as other people, especially boys, are concerned. "Mom, I have a mind of my own."

"But there are societal pressures," Mom said. "Look at books! Look at movies! Look at bathing suits! They all say the same thing: You are a body; sell yourself to the first comer."

I poured the Italian dressing on my salad. I like to leave it for last. "I'm not selling myself to anyone," I said. Then, even though I knew it was a delicate subject, I said, "Did you and Dad, um, do it before you got married?"

Mom looked embarrassed. "Well, we— No, actually we didn't." She took a sip of water. "Maybe we should have."

I wondered what she meant by that. I wondered if it had anything to do with what Dad had referred to, about his not realizing he really wasn't that attracted to women. "I thought you were brought up to believe you shouldn't do it before you got married."

"I was," Mom said, "but now I'm not sure. I still don't believe anyone should rush around doing it with anyone they're attracted to, but maybe, just to make sure . . . But then, who knows. If the marriage doesn't work, you look back and try to see if there was any handwriting on the wall. If it succeeds, you probably don't even bother."

I smiled at her, my heart thumping. "Next time you'll succeed, Mom, I'm sure."

Mom reached over and squeezed my hand. "Honey, that's sweet of you to say."

I smiled as I realized that at least she didn't explode and say there was no chance she'd ever do it again.

17

I set my alarm for seven o'clock Sunday morning. I wanted to make sure I was up before Mom to make the waffle batter and put the three letters on her plate. Making the waffle batter was easy. I pushed the thoughts of my last breakfast with waffles from my mind. I hadn't had much to do with Dad since then. I was just letting the situation stay as it was, and I guess he was too. I finished the batter, covered it with plastic wrap, put it back into the refrigerator, and got the waffle iron out. I hoped mine wouldn't burn and stick to the pan the way Greg's had. Thoughts of Dad and Greg together were the last thing I wanted.

Mom didn't get up until nine. I was sitting on the couch, reading, when she walked in. She was dressed. Mom never goes around in her nightgown or pajamas, even on Sunday morning. She gets up, showers, and gets dressed, just as though she were going to work. I ran over and gave her a kiss. "Happy birthday," I said.

She blushed. "Thanks, sweetie."

She followed me into the kitchen. "I thought I'd make some waffles," I said, plugging the waffle iron in.

"Wonderful," Mom said. "I haven't had real waffles since . . . Lord knows when."

She stayed in the kitchen while I poured the batter. "I never could get the hang of waffles," she said. "They always came out burned. My father used to say anyone could cook anything if they just followed the recipe. Of course, he never so much as boiled an egg, so what did he know? Anyway, I'm the living proof it's not so."

I kept watching the waffle iron nervously. It was smoking a little, but I know if you open it too soon, especially with the first one, it will stick. I'd remembered to oil the iron before I started. I was pleased. My first one was perfect, nice and brown and even. I put it on a plate. "You can start," I said.

"No, I'll wait for you. Let's cover them until you've done four. Then we can eat together."

In a way I wished she would find the letters and we could get that part of the birthday over with. Still, the waffles were turning out so well. Maybe that meant it was my lucky day.

When I'd done four, Mom carried them into the dining room. As she sat down, she saw the letters on her plate. "What's this?" she asked, in a friendly voice.

"It's sort of an extra present," I managed to say. "You don't have to open them now, though."

To my relief, she said, "All right. Let's eat these gorgeous waffles before they turn cold."

Mom likes honey on her waffles, I like maple syrup. I'd put both out on the table. "These are scrumptious," Mom said. "You're really turning into a fine cook." She didn't add anything about how that would make me a slave to some man. She just seemed pleased. "Now that you're here with me, it makes me realize how much I've missed Sunday mornings. There's nothing so dreary as waking up alone on Sunday with the whole gray day stretched in front of you."

"I like it too," I said. But my stomach felt clenched. I still hadn't gotten used to it. Even this morning when I woke up, I thought for a moment I was at Dad's.

Mom pushed her plate aside and reached for the letters. Under the table, I crossed my fingers. I watched tensely as she opened the first envelope. I'd put the man with the teenage daughter on top. Madge had said: Lead with your strong suit. Mom looked up, frowning, after reading the letter. "I don't understand," she said. "Who is this man?"

"Don't you want to read the other ones?" I asked nervously.

"Not until I know what I'm reading. Is this someone you know? The father of one of your friends?"

I shook my head.

Mom looked down at the letter. "It sounds as though he has some kind of . . . as though he intends or wants to start a relationship with me. How can he, if I don't know him? Or do I know him?" She looked at me curiously.

"He's just someone who would like to know you,"
I said desperately. "He's like you. He's divorced with
a teenage daughter my age."

"Is she your friend?"

"No, she, I mean he—" I began shredding my
napkin and putting little bits of paper in my lap. "I
just thought you might want to meet some men, some
nice men, so I put this ad in the *Voice*, and—"

"An ad for *me*?" Mom looked so horrified I got
scared.

"Yeah, only it was nicely worded. It just said you
were divorced and all and—"

Mom looked at me sternly. "May I see this ad?"

Trembling, I went into my room and got it. Maybe
I should have said I'd thrown it out, but I didn't think
of that. I handed it to her. When she looked up at me,
her face was bright red. "How could you do this?" she
cried. "I don't understand. How could you *do* such a
thing?"

"I—I picked the nicest people," I said, stammering.

"Do you know the kind of men who answer these
ads?" Mom said in that same shocked voice. "They
could be—anything! Murderers, rapists, madmen! How
could you do this, Nina? How could you be so insensitive?" She bent over and started to cry.

I felt worse than I've ever felt in my life. I went
over and tried to hug her. "Mom, I didn't mean to be
cruel. You don't have to go out with them. They don't
know your address or phone number. It's all done
through a box number. It's just Dara's mother, Madge,
has answered these ads sometimes, and she says— "

Mom looked up, hysterical. "Dara's mother! Is

that what you think I am? A promiscuous wildwoman who lets her daughter run around all night without any supervision?"

"She's not like that," I said. "Of course I don't think you're like her. I just—"

"But you want me to be, right?" Mom yelled. "You're ashamed of me the way I am. Well, *I'm* not. I'm proud of myself. I survived a divorce, and I'm raising you according to my own ideals and standards. I meet men like this every day, let me tell you. Mournful men with hard-luck stories who want me to raise their kids for them. Do you think I'm that naive? I want to raise one child, you, and I want to do a good job of it. I don't need these creeps!"

I took the letters and folded them in two. "Okay," I said. "To me these sounded like nice men. And I guess I thought now that Dad has someone, maybe you—"

Mom's eyes widened. "Duncan has someone? Who? Since when?"

My stomach plummeted. Why did I say that? "It's more a friend, really. He's more living with a friend."

"Which friend?"

I swallowed hard. "Greg."

There was a long silence. Mom looked straight at me. "I'm going to ask you a question," she said, "and if you lie to me about this, I will never trust you again."

"I—I won't lie," I said.

"Are Duncan and Greg just friends?"

I took a breath. "No, they're . . . they're a couple." I looked all around the room. "Dad said he's gay."

"Since when?"

"I guess since he was born," I said. "Only he didn't realize it until he met Greg. He said you shouldn't feel badly about your marriage breaking up because it wasn't your fault. It was more because—"

At that, Mom leaped up from her chair. "Oh, great. I'm so glad to know this. I, supposedly, have sat around thinking it *was* my fault, and now I'm let off the hook and so is he because—what? He was born gay? What nonsense! I can't *believe* he's been filling your head with such nonsense!"

I bent my fingers back so my nails could hit my palms. "He didn't say he was born gay exactly, he just—"

Mom was standing right in front of me. "Is this why you don't want to go there anymore?"

I felt really uncomfortable. "In a way."

"Why? Have they been . . ." Mom couldn't seem to decide how to finish that sentence. She looked as miserable as me, even discussing it.

"On Dad's birthday, Greg moved in. That was when he told me . . . maybe I just felt jealous." I was surprised I said that.

"You mean, he moved Greg in without even telling you first? Without asking how you'd feel about it?"

I nodded. I was glad she understood how I'd felt. "Uh-huh. I felt like maybe he should have asked me."

"Of course he should have!" Mom said. "How could he do a thing like that? Move a total stranger into the house with you, expose you to an unnatural relationship, rub your nose in it."

"Mom, Greg isn't a total stranger. He was there a lot before. I never minded that. Of course, I didn't know they were lovers, but he's not, like, a bad person or anything."

Mom's face was still flushed. "Why couldn't he wait until you were in college?" she said. "You're thirteen years old. You're far too young to—"

Even though I also wished that Dad had waited, I felt indignant that she regarded thirteen as that young. "I know about gay people," I said. "That doesn't bother me so much. Actually, I think I'd have felt even worse if he'd met some woman with kids who I would've had to get along with. At least this way I'm still his only child."

"That sounds mature, but I don't believe a word of it," Mom said. "You may think thirteen is old enough to do or say or know anything, but it's not. You're having trouble in school, you—"

I felt angry. "One class, chemistry, and I'm doing better. I was elected editor. I'm not some dropout!"

"The last thing in the world you need," Mom said, ignoring this, "is an unstable home environment like that. Thank heaven you had the sense to move back here!"

It's ironic that the one thing I did that I'm not in the least bit proud of, since I did it out of cowardice, Mom thinks is so great. How stupid to place that ad. Maybe being around Madge made me forget how totally different mothers can be. My main fear had been that the men might not turn out to be as nice in real life as they'd sounded in their letters. My mom hadn't even read the other two letters. I'd gone to all that trouble for nothing. Maybe if she hadn't been so wrought up about the ad, she would've reacted differently to the news about Dad. I wished I hadn't mentioned that.

"What a birthday," Mom said, looking down miserably. "What a present."

She sounded bitter. I felt really hurt. I had gone to a lot of trouble with the ad, wording it just right, weeding through the replies. "They sounded nice," I insisted. "I didn't know you'd take it that way."

Mom motioned at the letters dismissively. "Oh, I know, Nina. Your heart was in the right place. But that's what I mean. You have no sense of judgment. You're too young to know about this . . . That's why I can't imagine Duncan burdening you with his personal problems. I've always bent over backwards to avoid doing that."

"It's not a problem, really," I said. I wasn't sure which side I was on. Half of me agreed with Mom to some extent, but she was taking such an extreme attitude, it made me want to defend Dad. "Some people are gay and some aren't."

"It's a choice," Mom said, "like everything else in the world. I find men difficult, but do you see me rushing out and finding some woman to live with? No, I'll deal with my needs as best I can. I'll live alone, if I have to."

Why did my parents ever get married? How dumb I was to think they were alike. They're not at all, they're completely different. I'm still glad I was born, but I wish I could have been born to two people who got all this figured out ahead of time, before they started a family. "Mom, listen, Dad said he wasn't going to tell you yet, about this relationship with Greg. Could you not mention it if you speak to him?"

"Of course not," Mom said. "He's made his decision and now he'll have to suffer the consequences. I have no intention of speaking to him."

That wasn't what I meant. What if Dad called here for some reason to speak to me? "But if he calls here, will you not say anything about it?"

"I've given you my word, Nina," Mom said, leaving the room.

The letters were still on the table. I gathered them up and carried them back to my room. What a rotten birthday. I lay down on my bed. A few minutes later, Dara called. "So, how'd it go?" she said cheerfully.

"Terrible."

"What happened?"

I lowered my voice. "She won't go out with any of them. She didn't even read the letters, except the first one."

"Well, save them," Dara said. "Maybe my mom would like to try a few of them. But it's too bad, after you went to all that trouble."

"It was a stupid idea," I said savagely. I felt angry at Dara. It had been her idea. If only I didn't listen to her so much.

"No, it was a great idea," she said. "Your mom's just . . . too old-fashioned. But let her sit at home alone, then. Mom says everything in life is its own reward, and its own punishment."

"I shouldn't have told her about Dad being gay," I said softly. "That's what really got her upset."

"Boy, that *was* dumb," Dara said. "Why'd you do that?"

"I don't know. It just slipped out."

"Maybe you did it on purpose," Dara suggested. "Maybe you wanted her to know."

"Why should I? Now, even if I want to stay at Dad's again, she probably won't let me."

"I thought you didn't want to."

"Yeah, but I want it to be my decision."

Dara was silent. "I can see that.... Well, you sure didn't handle it well."

"If I hadn't planted that stupid personals ad, it never would have come up!"

Dara snorted. "Don't try to blame me! *You* thought it was a great idea last week. It's not my fault it backfired. Maybe she'll calm down. My mom flies off the handle lots of times."

"You don't know my mom." I felt terrible. I wished I could change everything back.

Dara was quiet a minute. "Do you want to come over here?"

Sometimes Dara can be totally understanding, practically one second after she's been awful. "I better not," I said, "but thanks anyway. It is her birthday."

"Well, don't take it so hard," Dara said. "And remember: She'll calm down eventually."

"Right." I felt better after I hung up, a little ashamed because Dara was right. Blaming her was stupid. Even blaming Mom. She just is a certain way. She can't help that any more than Dad can help being gay.

18

I didn't go to Dad's for two months and I hardly spoke
to him. I worked extra hard in school and tried to do a
good job on *Info*. Dara said I was getting to be a drag
because I didn't feel like going out much. On weekends, Mom and I were like two old ladies living by
themselves, sometimes eating out for dinner, sometimes going to the movies. It was gloomy. Mom got on
my nerves much more now that I didn't have any
contrast to her. She seemed pleased to have me working so hard, but I felt it was partly an excuse to avoid
thinking about other things.

One night at dinner, out of the blue, she said,
"Duncan is lucky."

"In what way?" I asked.

"I've been thinking about what you've told me.

He's loved two people in his life, me and Greg. I don't know if I've ever loved anyone."

I looked over at her, surprised. "You love me, don't you?"

"Oh, of course. I meant romantic love."

"Do you think that's important?"

Mom looked wistful. "I do. What will I do when you're grown and gone? I'll be all alone."

I shrugged. I hated her to say that. It made me sad. I was afraid to say, Maybe you'll meet someone. I wasn't sure that would happen to her. But Mom's bringing Dad up made me start thinking about him more. I remembered the fun times I'd had with him and Greg. I wished I could go back and redo my reaction to everything. But it all happened so unexpectedly. I remembered that night dancing with Stein, then being with Dad in the cab after the party. I guess I never wanted to notice, but there were clues. I didn't pick up on any of them. I was too dumb to see what Greg meant to Dad.

But I still didn't have the courage to go over to Dad's. I thought of it a lot, but it seemed much harder to reverse the pattern I'd set up.

School still kept me pretty busy. Damian and I talked to each other quite a lot now. I'd decided to run his piece on his gay brother, even though I knew it might seem a bit far out for our school. But I wanted to make a difference as an editor, so printing articles about things that I thought were important, not just trivia about how the lunches were inedible or the school dances didn't have the right music, was a way to come through on my promise. It occurred to me that I could have written an article myself on having a gay parent, but I didn't quite have the courage for that.

"This article is good," I told him after I'd gone over it for the final time and it was about to go to the printer's. "I'm really glad you wrote it."

He grinned. "Wow, praise from you! That's hard to believe."

I know I gave Damian the impression on our one date that I wasn't interested in him romantically, but he figured out that I liked him as a friend. When we talked in school, he realized I liked him and respected his writing. Still, I was surprised when one evening he called me at home.

Mom answered the phone. "It's a boy," she whispered, even though the phone was in the next room. I went in to answer it.

"Hi," Damian said. He sounded formal as he usually does. "Do you feel like going to another movie?"

He acted as if I hadn't seen any movies since that one night! In fact, I've seen ten of them. "I guess so," I said.

"Do you want to?" he persisted, as though that answer had been too uncertain.

"Sure."

"How's Saturday at eight?"

"That's fine."

"Should I pick you up at your father's, or where?"

"Oh, okay. Do you remember his address?"

"I wrote it down," Damian said.

After I hung up, I felt nervous. Why had I told him to pick me up there?

"What was that about?" Mom asked casually.

"A date," I said. "His name is Damian. Remember I mentioned him? He's in my class."

"I remember him," Mom said. "He's the writer, isn't he?"

I nodded. "It's a double date," I said. "Dara's coming with Tommy. I'll sleep at her house afterward."

"That sounds like fun," Mom said. She looked pleased.

I wonder why I lie. It seems like I lie even when it's not at all necessary. I could've told Mom I wanted to see Dad. She would understand that.

All during the week, whenever I'd see Damian, I'd wonder if I should tell him to pick me up at Mom's. But I didn't. I also didn't call Dad. I still had a key to his apartment.

When I got to Dad's apartment it was only seven-thirty. I hesitated a moment turning the key in the lock. It was quiet in the apartment. It hadn't occurred to me that Dad wouldn't be there. I'd thought of various other things, like whether Greg would have moved out, but not that no one would be around. Maybe they were out for the evening.

I looked around. Greg's stuff was still there. The furniture seemed to go together better than I remembered. I wondered if Dad had moved some of his belongings. It didn't seem crowded. Even though I knew I had a perfect right to be there, I felt funny, alone in the apartment. I sat in the living room, waiting for Damian, leafing through one of Dad's magazines, feeling as though I was in a doctor's waiting room. When the doorbell rang I jumped, I felt so scared. *Don't be a jerk*, I told myself. I went to open the door.

Damian looked the usual way, not that dressed up. I was glad because it made it seem less like a date. He entered the front hall.

"We can go," I said quickly.

"I thought I might say hello to your father and his friend," he said politely, looking around.

"They're not here."

"Oh. . . . Where are they?"

"I don't know."

Then for some reason I completely broke down. I told Damian about the whole thing, even about Mom and the personals column. I babbled on like a maniac about little details, like Greg's burning the waffles and how I'd lied both times about where I was staying. It was strange, because I don't really know Damian that well, but through his article I feel I do know him.

Damian listened thoughtfully. "It must have been a shock," he said. "I felt that way when I learned about my brother."

"What I don't get is why I lie so much," I cried. "Why do I?"

"I do that, too," he said. "Sometimes I can't help it. I get sick of my parents checking up on me all the time." He hesitated. "They don't know I'm going out with you. I told them I was going to the chess club."

I laughed nervously. "I can't even play chess."

"Neither can I."

For some reason that struck both of us as hilarious. We began laughing the way I sometimes do with Dara, in that helpless way when you're afraid you'll never be able to stop. Finally we did stop. "Do you still want to see a movie?" Damian asked.

"What else could we do?"

"We could just stay here and watch TV, if something good is on," he suggested.

Somehow that seemed spooky, staying in the quiet apartment, not knowing when or if Dad and Greg would return. Instead we looked in the paper and found a movie I'd heard was pretty good, *A Letter to Brezhnev*.

"It ought to be 'A Letter to Gorbachev,'" Damian said in his precise way. "It's outdated."

"Well, do you want to see it or not?" I asked impatiently. I still felt keyed up, having blurted out so many really personal feelings.

"Sure, why not?"

Walking there, I hoped it would be a movie Damian would like. Dara had liked it, but her taste might not be his.

The movie was excellent. It was about this English girl who meets a Russian sailor. The Russian sailor was played by an English actor who was really cute. He seemed fairly Russian, but not really. Anyway, her friend, who reminded me of Dara except she was supposed to be in her twenties, goes off with this other sexy Russian sailor and makes love with him. But the heroine just talks with her guy, even though they spend all night in a hotel room together. The result is they fall in love and promise to write to each other. At the end she decides to go to Russia and maybe even live there forever, because he's so much nicer than all the men she's met so far in England. I guess the moral of the movie was that love is important, maybe even more important than your family or your native country.

When we got out Damian said, "God, how stupid! Why should she go live in Russia? She was really making a big mistake."

"But she loved him," I said.

"So? She could've met someone just as good in her own country."

"But she didn't." I was surprised he could be so insensitive. It seemed like he'd missed the whole point of the movie. "She wanted to marry him."

"She hardly even knew him," Damian continued. "They'd just spent that one night together, and all they did was talk."

"I guess you're not very romantic, are you?" I don't think I'm that romantic either, but usually I can at least imagine what it would be like.

He turned red. "Well, maybe not. I don't know . . ."

We walked back to Dad's in silence. Suddenly I wished Damian was like the Russian sailor, someone mysterious and interesting, not just someone I went to school with every day. When we got to the door, he walked in after me. Before I could think one way or the other, there we were, in the apartment. It was still very quiet. "This is really creepy," I said. "I never thought they'd be away for the whole weekend."

"Do you want to stay here anyway?" Damian asked. "I can bring you back to your mother's."

"I think I'll stay," I said uncertainly. "Maybe I'll stay up and watch TV a little. They might come back."

"If you want, I can wait here with you," he volunteered.

I looked at him. I wasn't sure I wanted him to stay, but I also didn't feel like being alone in the apartment. I've stayed alone here hundreds of times, but because of being away for two months, the apartment seemed strange to me. While I got some sodas for us, Damian found a movie on TV, the late show. I was feeling really sleepy. It was one o'clock. "Won't your parents worry?" I asked.

"They think I'm at Glen's," Damian said. "He's the chess player!"

We laughed, but it didn't seem as funny as it had before, about the chess club. Two liars.

I must have been more tired than I realized. In the middle of the movie I fell asleep, not sound asleep, but I stopped trying to figure out the plot. It was something about gangsters with a lot of killing. My eyes were closed. Damian put his arm around me and, without even thinking, I leaned over against him. Gently he began kissing me, but I still half-pretended I was asleep. I was too embarrassed to open my eyes. I could even pretend Damian was someone else, a Russian sailor, someone mysterious and interesting. It was easier doing it that way.

When I finally opened my eyes, he said, "I wasn't planning on doing that."

"That's okay." I yawned. I hoped he would think I'd been kissing him in my sleep. "I feel so sleepy."

"Do you want me to go?"

"Don't you have to?"

"I could stay over here, if you want. Isn't this a sleep couch?"

I nodded. I knew it would make me feel better to know someone else was in the apartment with me. I decided not to tell anyone, even Dara, since saying I'd spent the night alone with a boy would sound much worse than it was. I went upstairs and got Damian a pair of Dad's pajamas. "So, listen, sleep well," I said.

He leaned over and kissed me. "You, too. . . . Don't be scared."

What would Damian do that I couldn't if a robber broke in, but it was more the idea that I wouldn't be alone. I wasn't really scared of robbers.

19

In the morning I woke up feeling strange, remembering how Damian had kissed me. I must be getting as bad as Dara, worse even. I didn't know I felt attracted to Damian until we started kissing. I hope he doesn't get the wrong idea about me, and think we're a couple now.

I showered and got dressed. But when I came down, Damian was dressed too. He was in the kitchen, making coffee.

"I guess they *are* away for the weekend," he said.

"Yeah." I got out a box of cereal. "Do you like Product 19?"

"Sure. . . . So, what're you going to do? Wait?"

I shrugged. "Maybe I'll hang around a little, till afternoon."

I watched Damian eat his cereal. "Listen, could

you not tell anyone—about staying over, I mean?" I asked. "I just feel sort of funny about it."

"Of course," Damian said. "What do you think I am?"

I wanted to add something about not saying to anyone we'd made out, but that seemed too embarrassing to talk about, so I didn't.

After Damian left, I felt better. Maybe because it was daytime, I didn't mind being alone in the apartment. I did some homework, I fixed lunch, I even called Dara. "So, how was the date?" she said.

"It was good," I said. "We saw *A Letter to Brezhnev.*"

"Oh, wasn't that great?" she said. "Didn't you *love* Peter Firth?" He was the one who played the Russian sailor.

"Yeah, I thought it was really good," I agreed.

"I wish they'd done more fooling around," Dara said. "He was so good-looking!"

"But that was the whole point," I said, exasperated. "They got to know each other better through just talking."

"Yeah, I guess," Dara said. "But I still wish they had— Did Damian try anything?"

"No!" It was true that he hadn't in the movie, so maybe that wasn't a total lie.

At around four in the afternoon, I heard Dad's key in the door. He came in alone. I was sitting on the couch, reading *The Odyssey* for school. "Neens!" he said, looking pleased.

"Hi." I had already decided to act as regular as possible.

"When did you get here?"

"Last night."

"You were here all alone? Why didn't you tell me you were coming?"

I shrugged. "It was kind of a last-minute decision. Where's Greg?"

"He's staying over another night at Myra's house on the Island. I felt like getting back. I had work to finish." He came into the room and sat down across from me.

Suddenly I felt really awkward. I flipped through the pages of my book.

"So, how've you been?" Dad asked.

"I've been okay. Nothing special."

He looked at me intently. "I've missed you."

"Me, too." I didn't look up at him.

"Did you feel frightened being alone? I didn't know you were coming. I'd have been here."

I hesitated. "I was fine."

Dad looked at me and then away. "Does Jean know you're here?"

I shook my head. "No."

"Why? Are you afraid she'll mind?"

"I think it's more up to me," I said.

"True." Dad looked wary. He tried to smile, but it wasn't his regular smile. "How's school? Are you enjoying being an editor?"

"Yes. I'm doing better in chemistry, too."

"I'm glad. It must be Jean's genes. I almost failed it myself."

"Jean's genes" sounded funny. "Weren't you a good student in school?"

"Not especially. Not as good as Jean. I was always tuning out. I had a lot of trouble concentrating."

"Sometimes I'll start listening, and two seconds later I'm thinking about something completely different," I said. He nodded.

"My best friend, John, was a much better student," Dad said. "I used to copy his notes almost every day. If it wasn't for him, maybe I wouldn't have made it through high school. I'm not stupid," he said, laughing. "I had a lot of trouble concentrating."

"It sounds like we're a lot alike," I said.

Dad touched the top of my head. "I hope you don't go bald at thirty," he said.

I reached over and touched his head. "You're not bald," I said. "I think you're good-looking. So does Dara."

Dad smiled. "Thanks," he said.

Our eyes caught, and held. "Do you want to come back?" he asked, his voice shaking a little. "The way we used to be?"

"I—I think so," I said.

Dad looked away. "Greg can stay with a friend those days, if you'd rather."

"No, he can stay here," I said. "I don't mind." Then I told him that I'd told Mom everything.

"What did she say?" Dad asked uneasily.

I decided not to tell him her first reaction. "She said she thought you were lucky because you'd loved two people romantically, her and Greg. She hasn't ever loved anyone."

"She loves you," Dad said, but he looked sad.

I smiled. "Yeah, I told her that. . . . She meant the other kind of love."

Dad came over and sat down next to me. "It was terrible when you moved out."

"I guess I needed some time by myself." I didn't feel like I could apologize. I just hoped he would understand.

"Is there anything you feel like asking me?" Dad said. "Anything that's been bothering you?"

I looked away. It was embarrassing, but I felt I had to say it. "I worry about your getting AIDS and dying. That would be so terrible."

Dad squeezed my shoulder. "Neens, the sad, dull fact is that I'm a monogamous guy. I was with Jean and now I am with Greg. I don't have a wild past. It isn't even the health issue, though of course I want to live as much as you want me to. There's no way I'm going to give up a chance to be a grandfather to all the kids you're going to have."

I looked at him in horror. "I'm not sure I'm even having any."

"Maybe not. But I want to be around just to see you grow up. All I ever wanted with Jean was what I have now with Greg, something that feels permanent and exclusive, just the two of us. Even if AIDS didn't exist or even if a cure for it was found, I'd be too nervous for a lot of one-night stands."

I laughed, relieved. "I'm too nervous, period."

"Take it as it comes, sweetie. You're still so young. . . . Speaking of which, how *is* Damian? Are you still going out with him?"

"I went out with him last night." I looked at Dad quickly. "Actually, he stayed over because I felt funny being alone in the house. Is that okay?"

Dad didn't even hesitate. "Of course," he said. "I hope he found the sleep couch comfortable."

"Yeah," I said, "he did."

That was what I liked in Dad. He trusted me, even when I didn't always act in a way that showed I was trustworthy. If Mom had heard I'd had a boy sleep over in the same apartment with me, alone, she would have raised the roof. Dad and I decided to eat dinner later. We can't go back, but we can go forward.

Later I told Mom I wanted to go back to staying with Dad part of the week. She didn't give me a hard time. One of her favorite expressions is that people never act the way you expect them to. It's ironic she says that because she's a prime example of it. Then she said something surprising. "You don't have to take care of me."

"That isn't why I was staying here," I answered.

She looked embarrassed. "What I mean is I know it would be easier for you in some ways if I'd met someone, the way Duncan has. I wish I would, too. Maybe someday I will and maybe not. But I know you've got your life to lead."

An image of Damian flashed in my mind. "I'm not about to get married," I said, smiling. "You don't have to worry about that."

"I'm not. I think it's that as a parent you want so much for your child—I know, you're not a child anymore, but even as a teenager—not to have to make the same mistakes you did. But even if kids don't, they have to make *other* mistakes. Everyone does. I've always liked this quote I read somewhere: 'Life is a circus without nets.' I wish there could be nets, for you anyway.''

I know what she means. Mom wants what's best for me. Now that I'm seeing Damian more seriously it scares me. The relaxed, easy way we were together when we were only friends is gone. Sometimes it's a lot better, a kind of all-out closeness that's really exciting, and other times, when we misunderstand each other, it's so painful that I can't stand it. "I'll be okay, Mom," I said to reassure her.

Mom hugged me. "I know you will." She looked up at me. "Tell Damian I really liked his article in *Info*. He writes well. That must have been a tough piece to do, since it's so personal and public."

For some dumb reason I reacted with jealousy. "Do you think he writes better than I do?" I asked.

"Of course not, Nina. Are you in some kind of contest? Can't you both be good?"

"Sure, I just don't want him to be better." I think I'm more competitive than I thought.

Dara was pretty amazed at first when Damian and I began being considered a couple. "I thought you'd be ninety-nine before you'd even look at someone cross-eyed," she said.

"Thanks a lot," I said sarcastically.

"I mean, I knew you *liked* him, I knew you were *friends*, but I didn't get the feeling it was really leading to anything more."

"We're still friends," I said. "He can get me mad just like you do. It's not like we're billing and cooing into the sunset."

She rolled her eyes. "That would be more than I could take. Give me a chance to get used to this, okay?"

I told her I would. What I like is that Damian understands that, even if we are a couple, I still need Dara as a friend just as much as I did before. And I think she understands that, just because I see him differently now, I need her just as much. I'd never want to have to choose, any more than I'd want to choose between Mom and Dad.

I see Damian a lot now at both Mom's and Dad's. Damian likes picking me up at Dad's because he enjoys sitting around with Dad and Greg, talking about ice hockey or baseball. But I think it's also that he's grateful to Greg ever since Greg got him an after-school job at one of his restaurants. Damian works in the front of the store where they sell pastry and cold take-out food. Whenever I go in there, he winks at me. "Hi, Beautiful," he says. He knows I'd slug him if he said that in school. He picked it up from Greg.

"Hi, Ugly," I say.

Then we grin at each other, and I go off to have a chocolate egg cream at the counter. Usually Greg is there, busy doing something. When he sees me, he waves. I've stopped having any special reaction when I see him. For a while when I saw him, it was like he had neon lights around him, "Dad's Lover," but now, like Damian, he seems like a regular person who just happens to be a part of my life.

About the Author

NORMA KLEIN is the author of more than 20 novels for adults and young adults, including *My Life as a Body* and *American Dreams*. A graduate of Barnard College, she lives in New York City with her husband. They have two college-age daughters.

Get your great
FREE
PAUL ZINDEL sampler!

Paul Zindel speaks the awesome truth — he writes real stories about real kids. Now you can get a free sampler filled with excerpts from nine Paul Zindel books:

Harry & Hortense at Hormone High
Confessions of a Teenage Baboon
The Girl Who Wanted a Boy
I Never Loved Your Mind
My Darling, My Hamburger
Pardon Me, You're Stepping on My Eyeball!
The Pigman
The Pigman's Legacy
The Undertaker's Gone Bananas

Just fill out the coupon below and get to know Paul Zindel — he understands you.

Bantam also publishes LOVELETTERS, a terrific free newsletter filled with the latest news about books and authors. If you don't receive it now, and would like to, check the box below. (If you are already receiving LOVELETTERS, please don't check the box — you are already on our LOVELETTERS list!)

- -